PURPLE TIES

ETSU TAYLOR

For James,

You've done so much for me, and you probably don't even know it, you've taught me how to believe in myself again when I didn't anymore, you've built me up, sparked something in me. So i dedicate this book to you because i know that with you by my side I can achieve anything.

Etsu Taylor

'EVOLVE OR YOU'LL BECOME EXTINCT'

PROLOGUE

Aria Creed was amazed. Despite everything, her school still managed to find a way to stay open. Despite the ongoing threat of dangerous criminals, despite the murders and muggings that had seemed to grow to be the norm news stories these past three months. Six stone high school and sixth form managed to justify their pupils attending *all* lessons like it was an average school year.

The fact that bloodthirsty criminals were on the loose all around the world seemed to have not made a difference. Of course, it did have something to do with the fact that most of the residences nearest the school now *lived* there.

To maximise safety, the police had ordered everyone to go to their nearest public building and hideout there, this meant that anyone near a school, supermarket, library etc. fled to these nearby acclaimed 'safe houses' and had stayed there for the past three months. The streets were off-limits until the authorities could get a handle on the threat that plagued them. Everyone was hopeful that that was going to be soon.

But Aria knew better, even though she belonged to Black Box academy now, she still had to keep up the 'I'm a typical eighteen-year-old' charade at her school with her mum and her school friends and this was getting increasingly harder to do when they all believed that the criminals were going to get caught and everything was going to return to normal. Aria knew better, along with the remaining academy members, Declan and Luke, they all knew that making the world safe again wasn't going to be that easy.

As much as everyone didn't want to admit it, the police weren't achieving much. The murders that were being reported daily on the news were mainly murders that evolved the policemen being killed themselves by the criminals that had been let loose by the end of the world.

All the news reports didn't say it was the policemen being targeted, no that wouldn't be good at keeping the citizens' calm and hopeful. The academy had been working overtime, day and night doing patrols and trying to capture and kill the prisoners before they found a way to get past the armed forces guarding the 'safe houses'. This was proving to be difficult as only thirty of the academy members remained after the prison battle the end of the world conducted.

Aria and Alice had been put in charge of the academy by Declan and Luke, who had been gone for the past two months. After a month of this continuous cycle of the killings and violence, it became clear that they couldn't win this on their own, so they had gone off in search for more people like them, people who had magic in their veins. Declan had said it was possible as, just like Aria, many people didn't know what potential they carried. They hoped to come back to Black Box with double the forces they had now. Aria didn't know if they could hold it together that long.

Even with the last few patrols she and Alice had done, it was apparent to see that the criminals were becoming restless. Most of the ones that had escaped out of hill view prison had stayed close to home. This, Aria could see, wasn't the healthiest move as many of the policemen that had put the very prisoners into jail had been killed and strung up on the fences and trees that outlined the border of the town. A warning, she guessed.

They were becoming more and more violent too, each day they would have to prepare themselves for the worst, and still, they barely got back alive let alone with their limbs intact.

It was official, Aria was sure, being mankind's perfect protectors was starting too well and truly suck.

CHAPTER 1
GOOD MORNING.

"Alice, everyone is waiting for you" Brendon's voice echoed from the hallway, only slightly muffled from the door that was the only thing that was stopping him from seeing the state she was in.

Judging from the full-length mirror that rested centre on the wall opposite her bed that she was currently sprawled in, Alice looked terrible. Her hair was knotted from where she'd tossed and turned all night, and deep, oval sized bags hung from her eyes just highlighting the almost too real and evident fact that she was exhausted. The past few days had left her drained and emotionally empty, this was mainly because the whole ordeal of running an academy was actually more stressful and time-consuming than anything she'd ever done. She had no idea how Jason had done it for so long and still managed to maintain his youthful appearance. Alice was pretty sure she could start to see wrinkle lines on her forehead from where she'd been frowning extra hard these past two months since Declan and Luke had left them.

That was something she couldn't help but worry about. She hadn't heard anything from them since they had gone off in search for more members to join the academy. Alice didn't want to think of this as a bad sign, she knew Luke wouldn't want her to worry but the fact that not even a letter or a single phone call had been made to ensure anyone that they were safe or at least still alive had sunk deep into her mind and waited there until she was sleeping too haunt her.

Aria was coping better than her with their newfound responsibility and Alice couldn't help but assume that this was her evolver gene helping her out in every way possible, anti-wrinkle abilities included. Aria no doubt was already out on patrol by now and even from the little light that shined, almost shyly through her closed curtains, it looked to be just past 6am, an hour she would've refused to be awake by if this was a normal day back when the world wasn't being taken over by bloodthirsty criminals.

Now she was a leader, and that involved attending academy meetings at ungodly hours of the morning. She sat up, the hair on her head fended off by an overaggressive tug of her hairbrush. Brendon's voice was louder now her hearing wasn't cloaked by her dreary sleeplessness.

"Alice? Are you alive?" his tone was more sarcastic than worried, and Alice pondered the question far too deeply than her sleep-deprived mind would've liked. She felt like a zombie, drained, ugly and 100% *not alive.*

"Brendon, I thought you liked me." She moaned, rolling to the edge of her bed and fighting the urge not to let herself continue until she fell out on to the floor.

"I do, but you're being silly," Brendon said, his voice sounding a little too smug for her liking. She got up and threw the covers off her. She was still dressed in yester-day's clothes; apparently last night she had been too dead to the world even to take them off. For a split second she wondered if she could get away with wearing them again today but her all too artistic brain stopped that thought before it could even be appropriately formed.

"The only thing that is silly is the time that I'm awake right now" Alice found a hoodie that wasn't too attacked by paint and a pair of joggers that were her 'I'm not going on patrol today' signal to everyone who would suggest that she should, Brendon being her main target.

"You're acting like we're not supposed to get up at 6am every day for training anyway, just because you've failed to do so for seventeen years does not make it my fault that you're bad at self-control."

"if I knew I was going to be running this place one day and getting up at 6am every day was going to make that eas-ier for me, I assure you we wouldn't be in this situation right now" Alice was halfway to the door now, opening it just in time to see Brendon roll his eyes at her comment. He jumped slightly but regained his composure enough to catch the chunky notebook that was crammed with notes and loose pages of drawings congregated over the past three months. He grunted as it landed in his hands but didn't complain as they started to walk down the hallway towards the meeting room.

* * *

Aria wasn't supposed to be enjoying it but going out on patrol every day was the only thing stopping her from leaving and going off to look for Declan and Luke herself. This was something she was close to suggesting to Alice, who was, she could tell, losing sleep over their absence as much as she was. She just knew she wouldn't let it happen, the academy's force was too weak for anyone to be going off on their own missions and with Aria being the only evolver in that force, she couldn't afford to be away from everyone just in case something big were to happen.

Like The End of the world coming back.

They hadn't been heard from since they disappeared through that portal three months ago, nobody had seen them, and not even anything on the news signified they were still around. Apart from the thousands of criminals still crawling, escaped into the world that they'd left behind, it was like they'd never been here or existed and Aria was happy to leave it like that if it wasn't for two things.

One is the fact that they promised they'd return to fulfil the Evolver prophecy and the other point being that when they left, they'd taken Felix with them.

Both things killed her to think about, mainly because the thought of the whole of the world's fate being laid solely in her hands didn't line up with her reality right now, which was that Felix was gone, Declan and Luke had run off and She and Alice were barely getting things together to keep the academy running, let alone making sure everyone inside it was okay.

The answer to that question was always in the range between, no and not really as Aria wasn't the most affected by her father's deaths as people had expected with her being his daughter and everything, in truth she was one of the only people in the academy who didn't miss him and ever since the day when Jason creed actually died the academy seemed almost dead itself. Nobody seemed up to doing anything, and even the routine patrols that were becoming part of their lives, where even the constant threat of death didn't even make any of the academy members blink twice. No one was passionate, no one was training as hard as they should be. It was depressing to see, but Aria felt like because she barely knew her father, barely knew the man that had touched so many of these people hearts, she felt useless in trying to heal their pain. She didn't blame Luke for leaving after all both his brother and the closest thing he had to a dad, had gone and nobody expected him to stay in a place where all the memories of those two people were prominent and still living so Luke had moved in with Declan, and soon after that they went on their quest to find others of our kind. Declan was also an evolver like Aria, and this was the fact that she clung onto when thinking of reasons not ditch everything and leave to find them. Declan would be good at protecting and keeping them both alive, he was powerful she'd known that the second she met him. She just had to have faith; they were both too busy finding people to help them to check up on everyone.

With all this swirling around in her mind, she didn't see the man coming at her through the gloom. He slammed into her so suddenly that her scream was muffled by the blow that blew all the air out of her lungs. She hit the pavement hard and automatically got her hands to her belt where she kept her sword. The man on top of her was trying to get to his feet, but the way he had fallen must've injured one of his legs because every effort he made to get up, he was brought down by a low hissing sound that showed that he was hurt.

Aria got to her feet quickly, no injuries, no pain. Her brain was buzzing, and she could feel her body reaching out to the elements, the air already coming to swarm around her.

She kicked at the leg the man was holding, although she couldn't see much in the low light of the morning, so her kick was more of a guess, it connected, and the man went down howling and cursing rapidly. She fumbled in the pockets of her jacket, bringing out a torch that she flicked on quickly, blinding the man in front of her and causing for the wild flock of pigeons on the street with them to scurry off into the sunset.

"You're under arrest, please don't try and get up," Aria said, her breath coming out in little white clouds in front of her.

The man was muttering to himself, and the only words she was able to pick up were "immortal" and "prison."

"What are you saying? I can't hear you" she was starting to regret coming out by herself, she didn't know what to do in these situations, normally the procedure was clear, you take them down, punch them a few times and then handcuff them but this seemed a little different and she wasn't good at making up the rules.

"I- need" the man's voice was rapid, and his breathing was heavy. Aria took a step forward slowly, trying to hear the man's silent ramblings. "– help me" was all he managed to say before breaking off into a wheezing coughing fit.

Aria frowned at him, in the darkness, it was hard to see, but for the first time, she took note of what he was wearing. It didn't look like the sort of thing a prisoner would steal from any shop or home nearby, the material seemed almost metallic as it shined in the orangey glow of the street lamps. It was all black, and despite her pre-thought notion, he didn't look to be in pain from the fall he'd taken when he crashed into her but from the massive jagged sized cut that ran the length of his right leg. It wasn't bleeding, but the metal clothing around it looked to be digging into the edges of the wound making it red, and Aria was sure it was infected. She gasped when she saw it and crouched down beside the man to get a better look at his face. He looked to be in his mid-20s, and He had a beard, black that matched his hair that was knotted and matted but still hung in curls in front of his face. His eyes were closed in pain, and as he laid there, quivering, Aria couldn't shake the feeling of recognition that hit her as soon as he opened those gorgeous blue eyes.

CHAPTER 2
SHOW AND TELL

Alice loved the meeting room, the walls were always finely decorated with paintings and artwork dating back for centuries. She had never really been in this room since she had become default leader of the academy, but now that she had spent so much time in here over the past few months, she was starting to, regretfully, hate the sight of it. It didn't help that there was often, like there was today, ten or so academy members screaming at her about topics none of them came here to talk about. At half six in the morning, this was something Alice, all leadership skills aside did not stand for.

So she was sat. Reading over the reports of the last week, hoping that if she ignored them, they would soon shut up. Brendon, who was, in his eyes, her right-hand man was standing throwing around hand gestures like they were solutions. None of which were helping.

She sighed, the headache in her head was starting to make its way down her neck, and she was sure if she didn't do something, this room and everyone in it was going to erupt in an emotional volcano. She wished Aria were here too hit everyone with a great windblast or at least a fireball, that would get their attention, but instead, all she had was a rather heavily packed notebook and a black ballpoint pen.

Alice stood, this action was ignored of course, and she couldn't let her thoughts of feeling like a year 9 maths teacher get the better of her as she slammed her hand down on the desk and screamed.

It was a passionate scream, one that seemed to break through the monotone sound of the other voices in the room. Everyone stopped what they were doing, and with a quick glance at Brendon, they all sat down into their seats.

"Right then, let's actually meet about something, not scream about it." Her voice was slightly sore, and even when she sat down herself, she could sense another wave of chaos brewing between at least five of her audience. She better get this done fast then. Alice looked at her list that had three main points of interest they needed to talk about. Brendon was looking over her shoulder, and she hastily brought her finger over one of the bullet points, she could see him nodding his head slightly in the corner of her eye, so she cleared her throat and began.

"Declan and Luke, we haven't heard from them in two months and three days. Many of you have requested that we make up a search party to look for them." She paused, letting that sink in. "now that isn't possible as you all know we have minimal numbers here and are barely keeping up the patrols with the numbers we do have"

People were starting to protest, and she had to raise her voice some more to keep from being drowned out.

"You guys know how much I would love to have Luke

back, but the truth is what if they don't need us to come looking for them? They could potentially be bringing us what we need. More members, more magic and maybe even more evolvers."

The room was silent again, and eventually, people were starting to nod their heads in agreement.

" The criminals are becoming more restless, and we need to put a stop to this soon, or they will end up getting into the 'safe houses', we know the armed guards won't be able to stop them if they work together."

"But you said it yourself, we haven't got the people to do patrols, how do you expect us to fight these people as well as keep a lookout" a ginger-haired boy she used to have dagger training with, spoke up. His voice was gruff, and as he spoke, she could see he was missing some teeth. She swallowed, sensing there to be an outbreak if she answered this wrong, she wished Aria were here, everyone was too infatuated with her evolver status to be upset with anything she said or did.

" I was hoping that Declan and Luke would be back with more people in time for us to do this, that's plan A, but plan B is more -"

Footsteps cut her off, they were loud, heavy and urgent. They stopped before the doors to the meeting room burst open, and Aria stepped through her face pale and stern. She was looking dead at Alice, her eyes sparkling with something more than urgency. Aria's gaze was soon brought upon the rest of the meeting's attendees, and she blushed slightly, the pale mask she'd had fading instantly.

"Alice, would you come outside for a second." Aria's

voice was cold, and Alice could see that she was shaking slightly.

Everyone was staring at her, and the sudden novelty of silence suddenly made her dizzy. Any underlying antici-pation was instantly cut off by the all too real urge to get out from under the hot spotlight that had been shining brightly on her before Aria had come in and saved her. The news she was about to share with her was something that seemed to have Aria conflicted as Alice could see in her eyes as she made her way to the meeting rooms door, that they were filled with the bright beacons of hope.

Aria shut the door behind them once Alice had made her way through, her short graceful movements were start-ing to make Alice feel sick, the nervous air around her seemed to make Aria uncomfortable as she began to too pace quickly down the corridor.

"Hey Aria, what's going on? Where are you going?" Alice shouted after her, bringing herself to match Aria's pace. They soon entered the cool, air-conditioned, front lobby that was quiet and empty, Alice noted that this was to be expected at this time of the morning.

"Aria? What's-"

Aria spun round to face her, her calm composure swept away by the sight of the man standing in the centre of the lobby. Alice jumped, not realizing that there had been an-other presence in this room apart from them. Whoever this man was, he seemed to have Aria in a weird sort of emotional panic.

"He – I – he bumped into me on patrol" Aria began, her breathing growing steady again.

"You found this man" Alice pointed at him absently "on

patrol? So he's –"

"Not, what you think" Aria finished her sentence, a slight burst of pity in her eyes that only now seemed to have washed over her. The man was still. Not fazed by their dispute.

"What is he then? Because to me he looks just like one of them" she said a little too harshly, but the sudden rage that should have come over her in the meeting room was seemly delayed until now. It seemed to be fuelling her, and in her groggy, tired state, she was willing to let it consume her.

Aria was shaking her head, and she stepped forwards towards the man and grabbed her hand so she would have to go with her. "Look at him, Alice, what is he wearing? Look at that injury, look at *him*" she said that last word like it meant everything, like the whole point of this interaction, was within it.

Alice followed Aria's gaze and found herself marvelling at how muscular he was, he was wearing, now she was looking hard at him, a sort of metallic suit that seemed to shine under the lights of the academy. The injury he had was massive, and Alice couldn't believe it hadn't been the first thing she'd noticed. It ran down the length of his leg, and the outside edges were blistered and sore from where the metal suit had been rubbing into it. It looked painful and nothing like anything she'd ever seen before.

Lastly, her eyes fell upon his face, which was, like the rest of his body, beautifully sculpted, his dark tousled hair hung in front of his face which was a mask of sweat and dirt. He looked older, his beard was black, and it snaked around his jawline and up under his nose. His mouth was held in a sort of tight grimace which meant to her that he was either trying not to yell out in pain or trying not to come and out say to her who he really was.

She was starting to see it now for herself, the reason why Aria was so rattled yet still so hopeful. She was beginning to realize why everything about him screamed at her, made her so angry. Her previous notion of letting it consume her was utterly cancelled out by the utter shock that slammed into her as the man that was stood in front of them gracefully but not intentionally moved his hair, so it wasn't covering his face anymore.

His Fluorescent blue eyes seemed locked on her face, while hers traced the outline of his. She didn't need to say it. She didn't even need to get a closer look. For she was sure that this man even though he was older now. Somehow, impossibly was her worst enemy.

Felix Quinn was back.

CHAPTER 3
(NOT) LIVING THE AMERICAN DREAM

"**n**othing is working, I told you we should be using hotel rooms, not trying to fit broken TV's in some rundown house in the middle of the desert," Luke Quinn said his voice only slightly louder than the car's low hum that seemed to dominate the other side of the phone call.

"Trust me, we don't want these people getting used to 5-star meals and comfort" Declan O'Connell's voice seemed to vibrate through the phone to him. "The house is fine, it's not like they'll be staying there for long."

"You're talking like we actually have people to be putting in these rooms," Luke said, his eyes fixed on the corridor of rooms they had at their disposal.

"We will soon trust me. Keep trying to find people and don't scare them off, you're daggers aren't as funny to look at as you think they are" Declan's voice was getting into that zone where he was starting to act like an adult. Luke didn't like that zone very much.

"Yes *dad*, you sound nearly as old as that car you're driving, how can you even hear me right now and dude, are you on your phone while driving?" Luke shook his head "tut tut Declan, what will the elements think about that?"

He could hear Declan snigger on the other end "hey don't diss the car, without it, you wouldn't be getting your weekly supply of cashew nuts or any food for that matter." The distant sound of the indicator ticked in the background. "And don't diss the elements, you know I'll be able to whisk you away in a hurricane in a second if I wanted too"

"That just sounds stupid."

"You weren't saying that when Aria *killed* an immortal, it was all 'Aria's amazing, I've never seen anyone do that' 'oh Aria this, Aria that'"

Luke closed his eyes, shaking his head again "oh, if it were you who killed Eddie, I would be saying the same thing about you, don't you worry."

"Yeah yeah and I bet if I had red hair and a great sense in fashion too, you'd be worshipping the ground I walk on"

Luke laughed. A proper genuine laugh, something he had not done for months.

"Come on Declan, you know I already do that."

Luke's bedroom was at the very top of the big house they'd rented out in the hopes to fill it with more of their kind. So far they'd found no one and Luke was starting to think that maybe it was because they didn't want to be found. He didn't want to think about the alternative, which was that there was no one else.

The top room of the house was good, it gave him space and when Declan was out on shopping trips like he was now it gave him even more time to work on his newfound *abilities*.

This was something he'd discovered two months ago, not long after the events at the prison, not long after Felix was sucked into the portal into nowhere. Ever since he had been brought back to life, things had been different, of course, they had been but not in a 'change my life for the better type way, this wasn't a mental change, this was something so wholeheartedly, and inexcusably real, because soon he wouldn't be able to hide it. Not from Alice, not from Aria and certainly not from Declan, who knew, he was sure, that something was up.

Luke hadn't been acting the most normal, and he'd hoped Declan would just pass it off as the side-effects of losing Felix and Jason so soon. This wasn't something he liked to think about, but when he did, it was usually the thing that set off this crazy new part of him. That's how he would describe it. It was a part of him, and he didn't know how to control it -

- His phone buzzed next to him on the bedside table. Luke had just taken a nap which had then resulted in two nightmares and a dream that reminded him all too clearly of the visit Billie had given him three months before. He still couldn't get the image of the vampire's fangs plunging into his chest out of his brain, even with all the meditation in the world he was sure it was tattooed onto the back of his eyelids.

He looked at the screen, rubbing his eyes to see the message clearly. It was another text from Aria.

'Hey, Luke? I know you need your space right now, but everyone is worried about you and Declan. I know I say this every time I message you and I just want to tell you that I won't stop until you answer me! So don't

think the silent treatment will be doing you any favours. But then if you really are in trouble then you'll be seeing me soon when I'll be saving your ass, so you really haven't got a choice, I'll be harassing you either way. If you're reading this message, then there is something you need to know ap-'

The text message vanished, and in its place, a number popped up. It was an unknown number, and Luke couldn't help but feel obliged to answer it. Aria's message would have to wait.

"Hello?"

"Hello, this is Mr Hunt, head teacher of Lasa high school. I was just ringing to confirm that your start date will be on Monday, please bring you're required paperwork with you."

Luke was stunned for a minute. "I'm sorry, I think you have the wrong number."

The man on the other end of the phone seemed agitated, but Luke could hear the faint tapping of a key broad in the background.

"Luke Quinn? We've had conversations with your guardian, Mr O'Connell. Were you not aware of this?"

Luke gritted his teeth, apparently his *guardian* had failed to mention this over all this talk of cashews and old cars. He cleared his throat "uh yes, sorry yep that's fine, can I ask what subjects I've been put down to study?"

Mr Hunt was silent for a minute before reading off the list of subjects he was going to have to endure. The last three in the list were what made him sit upright in his bed.

"Art, Dance and PE."

After the phone call had ended, Luke ran down the stairs of the house. It was a big house and very old fashioned.

The peeling wallpaper and the light littering of dust that seemed to be continually covering everything made him feel like they were back in the 1960s, which he guessed that was the last time anyone had lived here.

The kitchen was big, and this was ideal for Luke as he spent most of his time in here, not cooking- he left that to Declan but planning. A large map of America covered the middle table in the centre of the room. Bits were crossed and dotted in various spots, marking the places they'd been and had evidently found no luck in their search.

Declan's plan was apparent. Luke was to go to school. An actual high school. In America. Considering that Luke had never actually been to school before where you learnt maths and geography instead of how to use a spear too effectively decapitate an enemy. He could see many problems with the 'undercover' aspect of this plan. However, the naturally witty and good-looking part of himself should fit in quite nicely he imagined.

It was going to be an Irish magically inhuman boy pretending to be a hormonal, bored teenager.

What could possibly go wrong?

CHAPTER 4
NOT AS IT SEEMS

"**W**hy aren't you healing?" Aria questioned from the side of the bed she was sat on. The medical ward was typically always empty apart from the seriously injured patients, which with the criminals around seemed to make the ward teem with new life.

Felix was laid on the bed, his leg fully bandaged. He hadn't been talking much, but when he did, his voice was more profound than the last time she'd seen him. He was looking at her now, a sort of hesitant, reluctant look in his eyes.

"I haven't healed in a while," he said, his voice distant.

"What do you mean?" Aria asked, a noticeable questioning advancement in her voice.

"What's with all the god damn questions" he snapped at her suddenly. A sort of fiery glaze had joined the glint in his eyes, making the question hurt so much more than she'd expected.

"What?"

"Don't play games Felix" Alice said, gliding in from the hallway, two cups of coffee in her hands. She handed one to Aria, not looking at Felix as she took the seat on the other side of the bed.

"Felix?" his brow was furrowed, genuine question in his eyes, and it was strange to see at that moment because Aria had no reason to not believe his confusion.

"What's wrong with you? Did they do something to you?" she asked, getting up from her seat slightly so she could see him better, her eyes doing an automatic scan of his body, even though she knew that if the end of the world had done something to him, it would no doubt be inside his mind.

"Never mind that how are you here right now? The portal? –"Alice suddenly cut in. There was, despite the circumstances, a hateful glint in her eyes that Aria could see was solely directed at Felix. Aria knew Alice had hoped that the visitor they'd received had been someone else, but Luke Quinn's brother would have to do. For now. "The portal? - the portal" Felix questioned then a wash of realization rippled over his feature's. "What year is this?" he asked a soft uneasy tone in his voice, that if Aria hadn't been so instantly scanning his face in upmost confusion at this sudden change in mood, she wouldn't have noticed and as Alice answered the question in an even tone, she guessed that Alice wasn't so engrossed in the return of Felix Quinn, than she was.

"2020"

He cursed, putting his head in his hands. His fingers were gripped harshly at the roots of his hair.

"What Felix?"

"I – am – I haven't been here in a long time, I'm not meant to *be* here."

"What do you mean?" aria pushed, her voice high pitched

and unsure.

"I'm- I'm" he paused, for a moment catching aria's gaze with a short stern look, "from the future" he was looking her dead in the eyes and she couldn't help but be fixated by those blue iris that now seemed to have a reddish sheen to them that she hadn't noticed before and seemed to hold more meaning to her than anyone else. She looked, trying to see something in them that she was sure Felix was trying to tell her.

"Right and I'm an alien princess" Alice smirked, her eyes fixed on the coffee granules floating in the brown liquid in her half-full cup.

"eight years, i- ever since the portal, the last time I've seen you two was eight years ago it-"

"- what's going on? Why are you dressed like that?" Alice stopped him, the disbelief on her face. She clearly wasn't buying it.

"STOP" Felix throw his hands down on the bed, tears of frustration burning in his eyes. He shut them suddenly, screwing them together, his breathing growing heavy and uneven.

"If you're from the future then what's happened to us? The academy? Luke, Felix?" Alice had taken over the questioning and clearly wasn't fazed by the sudden outburst that seemed to be taking over Felix.

"Dead" he gasped, his teeth were gritted, his knees hugging his chest. The rocking of his body going back a forth was almost hypnotic, and Aria had to stop herself from wrapping her arms around him.

Her heart was pounding, and she was about to take a sip

of her now-cold coffee when a voice sounded that was so different from Felix's last, pain-filled gasp she had to snap her head up to meet his eyes again to make sure it was actually him.

He had stopped moving. His eyes had reopened, and his hands were back by his sides. Her stomach dropped as she saw the red haze in his eyes again that seemed to burn with hatred and anger. She didn't know what this meant, but her body was screaming at her, her evolver blood was telling her that the boy right here in front of her wasn't Felix anymore and the air around her seemed to pop in response to the cold, raspy words that he spoke next.

"You're all dead."

✳ ✳ ✳

Billie was soaked. The rain was lashing down on the streets, and she cursed the men who'd let her come alone. No umbrella and no car to travel in. Malus hadn't wanted her to cause a distraction, but Billie couldn't help but think that the blue of her hair that was being whipped around her face in the wind was drawing more attention to her than hiding her away.

Felix had been dropped here. She stopped letting the tracker re-centre and beep in her hand. Billie looked up through the rain at the long dirt track in front of her. If she had normal eyes, she wouldn't be able to see the hidden black building at the end of it.

The last time she was here, she intended to help them loose something. Now she was going to help them find it. Billie wasn't just here on a rescue mission, she was here to speed things up in the prophecy department that meant befriending the people at the academy, Aria, Luke, Declan and Alice in particular.

The only thing keeping her from killing herself right then and there at the thought of that was the fact that Eddie, her best friend, was going to be there with her. Even if he had taken over the body of her favourite brother. Felix was her key at getting the fourth evolver found and destroyed before any foretold battle could take place, and the destruction of the world and all the magic within it could come that little bit quicker.

Billie smiled to herself, and she began to walk down the path to the academy, surprisingly regretful that there was no one beside her to share her evil laugh with her.

You see, as amazing as the thought of killing an immortal god would've been for Aria and the others. It just wasn't as easy as that. Billie loved seeing the faces of all the people who had believed that even with all the power and energy Aria processed then, that she had enough power to kill Eddie, an ancient immortal being that ONLY the force of the four evolvers would be able to kill him. She just couldn't even begin to think of their level of stupidity. Billie knew they'd all put on a good show with the killing of Jason creed being the spectacle, and the portal being opened and Felix/Eddie running through to save poor old Alice from being taken. It was something taken out of a movie, and they all knew she just loved the drama.

But there was something so much more dramatic about that night. The feeling of knowing that not everything was as it seemed because Eddie couldn't just teleport himself, he could teleport other people. Over the years he had adapted that skill to not just being able to teleport physical bodies but delicate minds as well. So on that night, as soon as Felix had entered the proximity of the roof on top of hilltop prison. Eddie had swapped places with Felix in his mind so that instead of Aria's blast of power killing Eddie, it was killing Felix.

The Felix they knew and loved was gone, and the best part was they didn't know it and hopefully still didn't know it if Eddie was keeping his cover well. Her only doubt in her head was that wherever spiral had sent him in that time machine of his hadn't affected him too much, and she just prayed to the evilest gods that spending all that time in a body so made up of magic, Billie just hoped that Eddie hadn't started *like* it.

CHAPTER 5
THE GHOST OF THINGS YET TO COME.

Felix was laughing, his eyes darting almost wearily around the room as he did so, this was something, Aria was sure, she could only see, and it unnerved her in a way that she couldn't explain.

Felix was visibly older, his face was more structured, and his eyes held knowledge and history in them. As much as Aria would like to believe time travel was a myth and only something you saw in *Doctor who*, she couldn't deny what was right in front of her. Even the way he walked and spoke was different, and she knew if Luke was here, he would be able to confirm her suspicions that this wasn't Felix. Not as they knew him anyway. Aria hadn't known Felix long at all. Still, somehow in those days of being around him, she felt like she knew him enough to know that the slight reddish tint in his eyes had something to do with his 'non-Felix' like behaviour.

She was sat in the west wing library, the leather sofa's here were comfy, and she always came here to think. This wasn't going to plan as the blaring house music erupting through the speakers made it hard for Aria to even keep up a conversation. Everyone who wasn't on patrol was here too, although they were way more up for this party than she was. Something about forgetting about their duties and day drinking appealed to them, a display of moving bodies and thrashing arms and legs lay before her in the centre of the library. Cups of alcohol were littered everywhere, and Aria couldn't help but be jealous. Usually, she would be up there with them, partying with Alice, Brendon and Felix, after all this was what she had been waiting for, Felix's return back from the evil villains. But somehow she couldn't shake the feeling that Felix hadn't returned. Not the Felix she wanted, anyway.

She saw him then, his angular face staring at her through the crowd. She looked away, and before she could blink again, he was sat by her side on the leather sofa, his clothes, fresh from his wardrobe, smelt strongly of whiskey.

"How are you finding the party?" he asked, speaking loudly to be heard over the music.

"I've got too many things on my mind to be partying Felix." She said, not looking at him.

Aria felt him shift his weight slightly on the chair and lean in, so he was close to her ear. "A penny for your thoughts?"

She instantly got up from the sofa and with one defiant look at him, went to the glass double doors that opened up onto the black stone balcony that overlooked the county side. The cold air, set her heartbeat back to normal and the familiar tingling she always felt when she was close to the elements washed over her, her mind became clearer and the questions she'd wanted to ask as soon as she'd seen him in that alleyway poured out her mouth.

Of course, he'd followed her outside, and of course, he was standing there in the doorway of the library, his blue eyes scanning her body, impatiently like he was expecting something from her.

"What happened Felix? How are you from the future? Did the end of the world *do* something to you?" tears had welled up in her eyes, and she wiped them away before turning to face him. Felix shut the door behind him before making his way to stand a metre or so in front of her. He looked at her for a moment, and she realized she was close enough to see the careful glint of fear in his eyes. Whatever had happened in those eight years hadn't been peaceful, and she braced herself for his answer.

"I guess I should start from the beginning, with the portal" he paused "you will have to forgive me if my memory is a bit hazy, it has been eight years since I've brought myself to even think about that night."

"Why? Was it too bad to think about again?" Aria pressed. He chuckled, "it was too painful to think about again because it was the last memory I've had in eight years that wasn't filled with pain."

When he spoke again, his eyes were distant.

"When I went through the portal, the end of the world took me to this underground base, sort of like an underground bunker. They didn't do much and Malus and Billie slowly became obsessed with the idea of getting Eddie back."

The idea of that chilled Aria and a lump formed in her throat of the thought of the immortal she had killed three months ago. Felix continued.

"so spiral James came up with the idea of a time machine, as the body of Eddie was beyond repair, going back in time to get his body before he was killed was the only way they could think of getting him back. So-"his voice cracked, and she could see that he had closed his eyes.

"So they made me go into the time machine, on my own first, just to see if it would actually work. But um, but instead of taking me *back* in time."

"– It took you forwards" she finished, her eyes fixed on his face. "Felix, that's awful."

"When I got there, I landed in a room. It didn't look like anything special, and I remember thinking that I could just stay there until spiral James sent me back, so I did. I waited." His voice had grown solemn.

"Two days went by, and I knew that I was stuck, so I left the room and found that I was in a basement of some kind of where house. On the way up too, the surface I was walked past thousands of cells Aria. Prison cells. I didn't know what or who was in them until one cell I walked past shouted my name." he stopped and turned to her. "It was you, Aria."

Her breath caught in her throat. If she was in that jail cell, what possibly could've happened to her? Immediately her mind brought up images and imaginations of her years into the future, thinking of scenarios that could've got her arrested. These thoughts were washed away by Felix's soft Irish accent as he spoke again.

"I helped you escape in the end, it's a long story, and I guess you'll know it someday. When we were trying to get to the top, you told me that we were under the enemy's main base and that you had been captured for being an evolver. I told future you, who I was, what had happened and she told me that we were three years into the future from now" he pointed downwards indicating the ground below.

"you looked good Aria, strong, fast and your powers were insane, the Felix in that future fancied you quite a bit but he- "he stopped again. "He died."

"So three years into the future, the end of the world are capturing evolvers? And isn't future Felix you? You watched your future self-die?"

Felix looked at her for a long second and when he replied his voice was low like he didn't want her to hear it. "Not exactly" he looked up at her then, "the end of the world aren't the enemies, not anymore."

"But the prophecy did – "

"You won you and your four evolvers. And don't ask me who the other three were, I wasn't there when the battle took place and future you refused to tell me. The end of the world, three years on. Three years into the future are no more."

"Then who is it, who is this enemy?" her heart was beating so fast, and she realized she was gripping the side of the balcony with an iron grip.

"The enemy the world is facing isn't something I can tell you about, but we escaped the base and future you took me back to the academy. I can't tell you, but many things have happened, and three years into the future is just the beginning. I lived at the academy but in secret, only Aria, you knew about me, she thought about keeping me around with their actual Felix but that would mess up the whole time travel thing. You see, future you was set on helping me get back, we spent an entire year trying to return me. But then the war started. And everything stopped then.

"I've never seen such bloodshed. I've never seen such pain. The whole world was plunged into chaos, and I shouldn't even be repeating this to you, your future self told me not too, but during that war, all the humans were killed. She knew you would want to save them, but I am telling you 'The insane' didn't show mercy."

"the- the insane?" she stuttered on that word because the instant she said it, it sent shivers down the spine like in the edges of her mind her body already knew what Felix had seen of these enemies. What the world had faced.

"The insane is what we ended up calling them. I can't tell you anymore as you aren't even supposed to know this much." he sucked in a deep breath and looked out at the world around them. It was silent for a long moment before he spoke again.

"Five years, Aria. I fought for mankind, I fought for this planet. I fought by your side for five years. You must understand how weird it is to stand beside you now knowing that this world we are standing in, is going to change, that you are going to change and there is nothing we can do to stop it."

She was speechless. Any words to describe her reaction towards his story wouldn't have been enough. She just stared at Felix, not the Felix she knew but the Felix, her future self knew, and deep down inside her, she felt the distant pang of sadness.

Aria shivered again a sudden wash of sickness swelling up in her stomach, she went to get back inside when he grabbed her hand, stopping her from reaching the door.

"Wait - there's something more I have to say." His tone was desperate, his eyes were pleading, the red tinge in them still there but less menacing. "Thank you. Just know It was a pleasure to fight by your side, even if you-"he stopped, he was gripping onto both her hands now. He was shaking.

"Aria, just before I was transported back here" tears were rolling down his cheeks now. "Just before we were about too-"he inhaled deeply his sobs becoming uncontrolled "just before the end – something happened and you-"Felix came forward suddenly and wrapped her up in a hug, his head was resting on her shoulder and his sobs vibrated through her. Just when she thought he was going to pull away, he turned his head and whispered delicately in her ear.

"You died in my arms, Aria. I can't ever forget that."

CHAPTER 6
FIRST DAY AT SCHOOL. EVER,

Declan had dropped him off right in front of the school's entrance. Considering that Declan was only four years older than him, this wasn't something Luke felt he was obliged to do.

He had dressed to impress today and of course to scout out any potential of their kind they could take back to the academy or as Aria would say 'kidnap'.

The school day was dull, and nobody really spoke to him, more just looked at him from afar. The last lesson was PE. Now that lesson he was looking forward too. PE was essentially everything he was good at, running, jumping, catching, and throwing. Even if he was throwing and catching balls instead of knives and swords he was sure it was pretty much the same thing and, he guessed a perfect reason to see if anyone else processed the same skills as him.

So he got changed into some loose gym shorts and an equally as loose vest top and gathered in the gym like the rest of the boys.

"Right today boys, we're playing basketball" the coach shouted as he ran into the gym after them. The boys erupted into cheers and started barging into each other in excitement.

Luke could see that all the boys around him were athletic, but he was looking for someone who stood out from the best. They all looked similar and based on initial appearance, anyone in that room could have magical blood.

The positions were handed out, and Luke wasn't overly sure what a 'point forward' was or what he was supposed to do, but he was sure as long as he caught the ball and ran a little no one would notice. He wasn't here to be the best, as much as that pained him, he was here to find the best, and he knew he was in the right place to find it.

All the boys were on the court, and the coach blew the whistle. As soon as the boys around him started to move everything in his mind's eye went into a sort of slow-motion mirage, this often happened in a situation where his body had to be pushed to the limits, it was his blood's reaction to the elements around him. The gym had big windows at the top of its ceiling that were open, and the fresh air was slowly making its way down to meet him.

His movements were graceful as he ran past the rest of the boys still running in slow motion around him, the ball was in the hands of a tall boy who' hair was kept of his face by a bandana, and Luke had to resist the urge to rip it off his head as he shot over and snatched the ball out of his grasp. As soon as he did this, everyone around him returned too normal speed just in time to see him casually pop the ball into the net and land lightly on the floor.

The timer on the wall had only hit 5 seconds, and instead of playing on, they all stood there staring at him. Some of the boys had astonished looks on their faces. Others were seething with rage and jealousy. Luke couldn't help but love it.

The coach coughed behind him "come on boys, play on" he slapped Luke on the back, and everything went into slow motion again.

Luke's team won. The rest of the boy's thoughts on this were made evident by the deviant death stares he was getting from their rival team. The boys on his team were happy and kept hitting him brotherly on his back and chanting his name. Everyone but Ryan who was on his team too but wasn't so much as looking at him. Now Luke couldn't help but notice as he walked passed him on one of the benches in the changing rooms that he was holding his breath as he walked past. He knew that he was because the airwaves around his figure were pulsing and moving in a rapid sensation and of course he couldn't feel Ryan's breath like he couldn't other peoples. This was one of his new alibies he'd been getting used to these past few months. He couldn't help but feel like a freak, like what his body was learning to do wasn't normal for his kind. But in times like these, he was grateful for his magical advancement as this odd behaviour from Ryan then painted him out to be a person of interest.

Declan would be proud.

So instead of walking on, Luke stopped. Waited to see if Ryan would let out his breath or go to take another one, he didn't, and even though Luke wasn't facing him, he could feel the tension in Ryan's body as it struggled for air. It was really quite silly, the definite struggle Ryan was dealing with for reasons Luke couldn't wait to know. He turned to face Ryan, he kept his face neutral even though he wanted to grin at the possibility of something odd taking place. He used the three steps it took to reach

Ryan, still suffocating himself to death on the bench, to think back to Ryan's performance during the basketball game. It took him a second to place him on the court but he was sure he'd been the boy who actually was able to score a point for their team instead of Luke. That was something in its self because as much as Luke was undercover, he wasn't going to play nice or go easy on any one of those boys, so the fact that Ryan had had a breakthrough moment while Luke was there meant something magical was occurring. He hoped it was that and not just that Ryan was better than him as a human.

He sat next to Ryan and instantly saw him turn his head to the opposite side and let out his breath. Luke couldn't grasp as what he was doing or what it meant, but sooner or later, this kid would have to speak to him.

"You were pretty good out there dude, maybe you could join the team" Ryan suddenly said next to him, his previous weird behaviour gone and replaced with an air of conscious confidence.

"Yeah, maybe I'll come to the next practice." Luke said grinning at him.

"Cool," Ryan nodded.

Luke needed to get more out of him, after all, the longer he was here, the worse the situation at home got.

"You've got some pace on you," Luke said, trying to sound like he knew what that meant.

"As do you," Ryan said, not looking at him.

"Were you always like this, this good?" Luke pressed. He wasn't good at being implicit.

"Like what?"

"I don't know it's like you had magical basketball powers or something" Luke had really blown it now but how Ryan responded to this was important.

"Yeah well, I train hard, that works some magic."

Ryan abruptly got up and stormed towards the changing room doors, judging by the hard slam of the door behind him, Luke had ruffled some feathers. Which was strange because for all Ryan knew he was just trying to be funny. Friendly. Nothing about the conversation seemed threatening to either one of them. The way Ryan had left made it seem like Luke had straight up just asked him if he could fly and shoot lasers from his eyes. If it hadn't been for the inhuman way Ryan had moved out there, Luke would've just put this unusual behaviour down to hormones or something.

Ryan was one of them. Whether he knew it or not and this was something Luke wasn't going to let slip from under his grasp. Luke wasn't good at persuading, but the general term of kidnapping was the only way he knew how at getting people to do what he wanted them too.

CHAPTER 7
THE BASEMENT.

"What's our next move then," Aria said, she was sat in one of the chairs in the meeting room, Alice and only Alice was sitting opposite her at the big oak table. She was thankful for the lack of people in the room because she was afraid that if there was anyone else, she wouldn't be allowing herself this time to have a breakdown. She was shaking, and she had been since leaving the party in the library upstairs. Alice was, thankfully, still sober enough to recognise that this wasn't a good sign.

Alice was looking at her, still in shock at what Aria had just told her about Felix and their future self's. Aria didn't know what they should do with this information. What Aria should've done, she couldn't keep it to herself, and she thought that telling Alice would open up their opportunities. still, Alice was about to hit the panic wall that Aria had collided with already, and she didn't know if she could snap them both out of it.

Aria was in control of the whole academy, in charge of the safety of the humans now. She was the third evolver, she was meant to be protecting everyone. At least she had the knowledge from Felix that the prophecy, that the end of the world would be defeated by her hand but, she couldn't help but wonder, at what cost.

'The insane' Felix had called them would show 'no mercy' and Aria just couldn't comprehend the scale of violence that entailed. He said he'd been fighting by her side for five years against this new enemy, what the future held for everyone wouldn't last that five years.

She couldn't get the pain and sadness that was swamped in Felix's reddish but still beautiful blue eyes out of her head. It would break her heart if she kept drawing her mind back to it. 'You died in my arms aria, I can't ever forget that'- as much as she knew what the words meant, she just couldn't imagine what would have brought her to that point.

The fact that both she and Alice knew now was that they may have control over the academy and therefore everyone in it, they didn't, couldn't have control over the events that threatened the next sixteen years of their lives.

"We need a break" Alice's distant voice broke Aria's car crash of thoughts.

"What? We can't just take a break."

"Of course we can, everyone's drunk or having a good time upstairs, who says we can't do the same. Aria I've been promising I'd take you to a gig since I first met you, this is our chance to live the lives of teenage girls again."

Aria thought about this, Alice was right, everyone wasn't in the state to be making plans and Aria needed something to take her mind of the most recent events. She signed, nodding her head slightly and giving Alice her best teenage girl smile.

"Fine, what are band are we seeing."

* * *

Billie hadn't liked nearly being stabbed to death on her way to the new and 'top secret' gig venue and bar, given the fact that the crazed prisoner couldn't of known she was immortal and that trying to stab her would only anger her. That prisoner in question no longer had a face, and she had discarded his stabbing hand into the basements bathroom sink.

The steps down to the basement were slippery from the rain and Billie couldn't help the smile that hit her when her eyes were cast upon the chaos in front of her. About 200 people were jumping up and down, and the smell of sweat and alcohol in the air was almost unpleasant. Almost.

The music being played by the band on the stage was captivating, and Billie couldn't help but bob her head from side to side. Her eyes scanned the small room in front of her, which was filled with humans and not the magical kind. It was weird being around this, considering that she hoped most of them would be dead or suffering at the criminals she and the rest of the end of the world had left behind.

The specific redhead she was looking for wasn't here yet, but she was on her way, even with the hectic vivacious noise-blocking her senses the evolver blood was so distinct she was sure she would be able to feel it even when she eventually died. She would just have to wait.

＊ ＊ ＊

Declan O'Connell was hot, tired and unusually unaware. The streets of America, Texas to be exact wasn't a place where he would expect to stumble upon gold. Not the gold you would imagine in cowboy films, not the stuff you'd find at the end of a rainbow. No, the gold he stumbled upon was gold of the magical kind.

The rundown motel attracted him purely because it had a sign out the front of it that read 'we have what you're looking for' and ironically enough that very motel *did*.

Declan wasn't one for using his evolver abilities to 'sniff' people out but as soon as he drove into the motel's car park, his senses were sent into overdrive. He could feel the magic, he could feel elements responding to it. It was like rain in the desert. He just had to figure out where these people were because judging from the dilapidated roofs and rusting door handles of this motel, they weren't staying in these rooms.

His search brought him around the back of the building where the door to the basement was, this by chance was the only thing in the vicinity of the motel that had any traces of it being used recently. The hinges weren't rusted, and the doors weren't caving in and weak when he bent down to open them. They were a little stiff and creaked when they were moved. The dark hole that was presented to him was a surprise and the quietness that came after filled him with a sense of eeriness that didn't just make him want to run back to his car and zoom of into the distance it also made him feel ashamed of even thinking of such a thing. He was an evolver, however many of his kind were down here they would have to play nice out of respect and/or terror. Declan knew he wasn't scary, but he was hoping the legend and stories surrounding the stigma of the evolvers would be.

The dull light of sunset didn't do much in lighting the way down the stone steps, so Declan had to make do with the lighter he had in his back pocket. He flicked it on and brought his hand up to it, feelings the flame warmth and how he should connect with it. Within seconds the flames were dancing between his fingers and the area around him was lit just enough so he could see 4 or 5 steps in front of him.

The air change was almost sickening, it was as if he'd plummet 70 ft. as soon as he took a step down. It was only then that he realised that the dim light of the day that had been behind him a second ago was now replaced by a thick blackness that he was sure was a wall behind him.

The way in front of him was still dark, but the accents in the shadows were lighter, and he could tell as soon as he reached out to all the earth and dirt around him that he was in fact very deep underground. This wasn't a surprise to him as this sort of trick was close to the one he used to hide his home at the bungalow although this one didn't evolve drinking any elixirs of any kind, he was curious and pleasantly encouraged that he was in the right place. His doc martins weren't thanking him for the mud and dirt being rubbed onto them, and neither were his feet which were growing blister by the second. Declan's shirt was white, and he knew that when he left this place, it was going to be a whole different shirt.

It wasn't until he was a good 30 metres down the dirt corridor that he heard people approach, it was also around that time where big steel lamps were placed on the walls casting big winding shadows onto the floor next to him. Declan decided to stop walking and prepare for a commotion as soon as the people he could hear came into sight. He could feel their presence they were getting close and the magic within them wasn't necessarily powerful, Declan guessed they were teenagers, he didn't get his gun out just yet. They properly already knew he was here, and everything was going to be fine.

CHAPTER 8
EVERYTHING WAS NOT FINE

Everything was not fine. Aria was only 20 meters down the road when the criminal jumped her. Alice was some ways ahead, too keen and excited to get to the gig that she didn't even notice the sudden torrent of wind that slammed into the prisoner's ribcage behind her sending him flying over her head. She'd brought out her dagger and finished the job. Now she was running, which was never fun, and Alice seemed to always be faster than her even in heels. Alice's heeled boots weren't just for fashion purposes; they did have a violent quality, and Aria saw all too much what the sharped ended heels could do all too often nowadays.

They were running because it turned out that the prisoner aria had killed, had a fan club and now 20 or so criminals were chasing them down the road. Alice was laughing, and Aria was trying not to fall over her own feet while shouting commands at Alice who was, she knew, not listening.

The basement was coming up, and they both knew they couldn't lead the criminals to the room of innocent people down there. They were outnumbered, but that didn't mean anything, after three months of learning how to fight these people, taking them down was becoming second nature. They stopped and turned to the mob. Their eyes were seething in madness, and they all weren't directly looking at them, more off centre like they were scared that if they did look at them, they wouldn't be able to kill them.

Alice wasted no time, and before Aria could blink, she'd thrown a dagger through the man closest to her's head, and he'd fallen to the ground. The others didn't even flinch at the sight, and Aria closed her eyes and opened her hands so that her palms were facing the sky.

The earth around her latched onto her energy, she could feel it grabbing onto her, every single cell of the earth was responding to hers. Suddenly the ground, grass, pavement, and the whole space the criminals were standing on collapsed in on itself. Arias' hands were shaking, and she could feel her power growing, the magic wanting to go beyond just her but she couldn't let it, last time she'd let just a little bolt escape she'd managed to kill an immortal and caused a whole range of chaos. She'd be practising with Declan before he left on keeping it all contained and that's what she did now. 3 deep breathes, and the tingling feeling was gone. The ground in front of her was back to how it had been a minute ago, just a few cracks in the places where the pavement had broken. The inmates were gone. Buried. Dead.

Alice looked at her for a second and Aria could sense she was going to say something but instead she reached out and grabbed her hand. Alice out of everyone was the least bit surprised by Aria's growing power, but she did know how much effect it had on her when Aria did use it. Physically she felt fine, but mentally she felt awful regardless of how much the people she'd killed deserved it.

"If only Luke was here to see that." She laughed, dragging Aria, so she was walking alongside her again. "He would hand you his ego on a plate."

Aria smiled. She hated to think about Luke and especially about the parts of him she and everyone around him loved. She didn't think she could miss the presence of someone and still find it hard to remember it. Aria knew that regardless of how long she'd known him, irrespective of his absence. She couldn't get over the feeling she felt when she knew wholeheartedly that he had been dead, it had broken her and even though she'd known him barely a day at that point something inside her felt all the pain like she'd known him all her life.

So all she could do was smile. Alice was sharing her pain and actually being someone who had known Luke her whole life, she was acting more rationally than Aria ever could.

"Don't you think it's weird" Alice spoke again, a new hint of curiously in her voice that brought the flock of butterflies in her stomach to begin flutter slowly. "So Felix has lived in the future for eight years. And you would think that now he's back that he would ask about his brother because I don't know about you but before... everything, they were inseparable and when Luke .. Died he was destroyed, right? Surely living life in the future and then coming back after so long you would be dying to see someone you loved so much." she stopped, letting the thought trail off.

"Yes, I did think that." She said, keeping her eyes on the horizon in front. "He hasn't once asked where Luke is or anyone for that matter. I didn't really take note of it before but Alice, don't you think he's different and not just 'he's older now' different like he's completely different. Not like Felix at all."

Alice didn't say anything for a while before she whispered into the cold evening that surrounded them "what if it's not Felix."

Aria shivered at the thought but didn't completely dismiss it after all this was the infinite ending too all her suspicions. What if the end of the world had done something to Felix or more suspiciously what if spending ten years in the future had somehow changed who Felix is? She felt sick at the thought of it, and once again she found herself wishing that Luke was here with them.

* * *

Everything was not fine. The truth. That's what it was. He'd just blurted it all out. He was stupid, of course, to have done that in such a fragile part of the timeline, but he couldn't help it. Being around her. Being there with her so soon after she'd left him.

Of course, she didn't know how much that time had meant to him. How much it will mean to her eight years into her future. It was so strange to be back in a place so simple yet so heartbreakingly different. It was weird to be in the academy as Felix, as the boy who was the best at everything, the boy who had the golden brother. The boy who was strong, fearless and inexcusably allowed to be himself.

He didn't have to hide. He didn't have to sneak around. He could be here and be himself. Which was, Felix Quinn. He was him. That was something he knew he'd have to explain for he knew now that back in this time, this year. The end of the world were the biggest danger, the danger he was once a part of, and he guessed he was still expected to be a part of it. They could come looking, and he knew Billie would be the first to find him. She wouldn't understand, of course, because she didn't know what it was like to be one of them. To have magic in your veins that, allows you to become the better version of you.

They all wouldn't understand, they would kill him if they knew he was well and truly Felix Quinn. Because even though he'd lived ten years into the future, even the he'd fought and killed alongside the academy and more importantly Aria creed. Even though he was expected to live in a body of someone so different from him. He just couldn't help but feel at ease. Like he was finally the person he was meant to be.

Thinking back to the time where he had just entered this body, he'd hated it. Hated the way it felt and he hated the way everyone looked at him. The magic made him feel sick at first, but once he'd stepped into spiral James's machine and walked out into a world so different to this one, he couldn't help but think that was the making of him. The making of Eddie. The bad guy who had evidently turned good.

So no, everything was not fine. Aria knew about the future, and he could see it in her eyes that she was suspicious or unsure of him. She wanted to believe that he was Felix but the look she'd given him in the medical ward the second he'd told them they'd all died. That look was something close to regret.

Everything was not fine if Billie and or the rest of the end of the world came looking for him, which they would be by now. Everything was not fine if Aria and the rest of them find out who he really is and everything was well and truly NOT FINE as of now.

Eddie was in his room. The white walls and soft linin sheets were sprinkled with little sections of Felix. Band posters and weapons, video games and pictures were everywhere. But that wasn't what he was looking at. He was looking at himself. At his face.

But most importantly, he was looking at the one-half of his eyes that were turning a molten red. The colour was bleeding into the blue of his iris as if someone had slashed them with knives.

It was fascinating but oddly horrific at the same time, and Eddie wondered how long they'd looked like that. No wonder Aria had been having a hard time believing he was actually Felix.

As he looked deeper into his irises, he could see a faint line of purple appear just as the red and the blue mixed. That colour not only marked him out as different, but the purple also tied him to his new life and signified the change, the end of an era.

❊ ❊ ❊

Everything was not fine. Declan had been thrown to the ground and was now being retrained so tightly that he could barely move his pinkie finger. The ropes that bound him had some sort of substance on him that dulled the magic inside him. This was probably a good thing because as any evolver will tell you being retrained with all that power inside you, being able to manipulate the elements could be a very dangerous thing, especially in enclosed space.

There were five or six teenagers at the driving force of the attack, and Declan had been so focused on the ones approaching him he'd not seen the ones behind him.

So now here he was being pinned to the ground by some kids 5 years younger than him, and he couldn't do anything about it. When he tried to speak they would just speak louder if he tried to move they would kick him. He hadn't done anything wrong in his eyes but the violent welcome he'd been shown just concluded to him that they hadn't had anyone down here in a while.

He didn't know if they knew he was an evolver and even if they did it didn't seem like they cared. They had started to bring him up so he could walk upright. They all surrounded him and were pushing him forwards down the dirt tunnel some more. It had gone quiet due to the amount of concentration they were putting in trying to get him to stand so Declan saw this as his only chance to say his peace.

"I come in peace, honestly is this all necessary?"

The one closest to him responded, and he couldn't see his face because it was masked by the hood of the cloaks they all were wearing. "You're an evolver, you cannot be trusted."

Before he could reply he was brought into a room. The contrast from the small dimly lit dirt hallway to this wide-open cavern was fundamental in distracting Declan from where he was, he could feel the earth and the rocks, stones, leaves, dirt everything was amplifying his energy his powers, his desire to thrive, the tingling in his hands was electrifying and just before it all came too much, he sucked in a breathe waited and let it out slowly. He hadn't realised he'd shut his eyes and when he opened them he was suddenly surrounded by masked people, the open room they were all stood in was cave-like but surprisingly warm and homely. Lights twinkled down from the roof and quaint pictures and decorations littered the rocks and walls. A man was stood amongst the crowd, not on any throne or anything, not with anything to mark him out as the leader apart from the fact that he was the only one not wearing a mask. The man's face held no clue as to what he was thinking or if Declan was going to be punished or congratulated for being here and for being an evolver. Declan hasn't realised that the masked teenagers guiding him to a stop in front of the crowd that had gathered had let him go, and he was now free from any prior restraint. That was a risky move on their part, but something about the way the unmasked man was looking at him told Declan that maybe it wasn't so risky after all.

"Young evolver, what brings you here today?" the old man said, his voice gruff and dry but the walls carried it as it echoed lightly around the room. Declan smiled at the man, rubbing the dust off his clothes and clearing his throat even though he didn't need too.

"My name is Declan O'Connell and I'm here today because I need your help"

CHAPTER 9
THE DEAL.

The basement was rammed full of the sneaky rule breaking humans who sneak out weekly to this hidden away venue and enjoy themselves. At first it was only meant to be a youth centre for the children to have a safe place to play but as the months of the criminals got worse Alice had seen many more adults attending and drinking to get their minds off everything. She didn't blame them after all she was here most weeks, not that aria knew anything about it.

It was a small room with steps leading down into it, the stage was set up with the bands equipment and the bar was barely 2 metres away from it. The bar tenders and band members were the only people in that room, apart from Aria and Alice, that were from the academy and that meant that even though they weren't technically on patrol, the fact that they were here with the humans and ready to jump into action as soon as anything dodgy happened, put Alice's mind at ease because they *were* looking out for the humans just with a few more shots of vodka than normal.

"Who's playing tonight?" Aria asked squeezing past a drunken group of teenage girls that were two drinks away from stripping naked and dancing on the bar. Alice smiled, "I think they're called criminal justice tonight, they change their name almost every time but this band is the only band that plays here."

Aria nodded not letting the smirk that was trying to insert itself on her lips win. She wasn't letting herself take her mind off everything and that wasn't the purpose of the break. So she grabbed her wrist and lead her over to the bar area. Which as much as Alice would've liked wasn't full of handsome men reeling of their endless scripts of pickup lines. No this bar was run by no one other than Brendon. Who was only useful in this circumstance for giving them free and strong, Alice always insisted, drinks.

He looked flustered and beads of sweat were raining down his forehead. Brendon looked at them and not too sure whether to wave or cry in relief he came over and lent over the bar to talk to them without anyone hearing.

"Alice, I swear to god, I keep breaking the glasses out of stress." His voice was shaken and Alice had to bring herself to not laugh at his struggles.

"Don't blame your strength for you lack of control and anyway didn't I say you'd have a chance on stage tonight if you did this."

Brendon nodded, and aria looked at them both "he's going on stage tonight? Doing what?" the shock on her face was comedic and once again Alice had to hold in her fits of giggles.

"Well Brendon has wanted a chance to shine on the stage for ages and I thought that if he took over bar tending duties while Lester is on patrol tonight, the band will let him have his moment"

Brendon was flushed but cleared his throat to sing, Alice put her hand on his mouth before a note left it. "Save your voice for the stage. Please."

"So you sing? I thought you were more of a piano player or a violinist." Aria was laughing next to them. Her eyes were lit up in little balls of power and light which always happened when she was in an intense environment. She often had to wear contacts when she went to visit her family and friends at the school to keep any suspicions about her away. Here people were either too drunk to notice her or too caught up in the music too care.

"Aria just because you can throw fire balls doesn't mean you can make jokes about my hobbies, I've been singing since I was eight and it's been my dream to take it to a stage. Anyway didn't you say I would be 100% singing tonight you don't seem very confident?"

Alice cleared her throat. "Well I said that you'd cover Lester's shift. And if Lester isn't here he can't object to someone going on stage and singing for a bit."

"So you didn't ask Lester and you aren't sure if I can actually go onstage. So I've been serving drinks for hours for no reason"

"Hey Brendon, chill, you'll get your chance. We'd better get to the front so we can see the band clearly."

Without letting Brendon mouth a reply, Alice dragged aria threw the crowd to the front by the stage. It was hot and sweaty and the atmosphere were electric, prosberly due to the storm brewing outside. Aria was fidgeting next to her and alice had spent enough time with her over the last three months to know that this was the result of the large elemental activity outside. Its power was racing through her and she had no doubt that if aria wanted too she could kill everyone in this room with the click of her fingers. Alice just wished that when the battle the 3rd evolver prophecy foretold finally happened it would happen when a storm was brewing.

"do you think The end of the world are here?" aria asked randomly. Alice shook her head about to shut down her attempt at stirring the conversation to work related problems when she saw a flash of blue hair skim through the crowd, 5 people to their left. She paused trying to work out weather the stone dropping feeling in her stomach was due to the question aria had asked or the fact that the question aria had asked had just be been answered for her.

* * *

So they weren't drinking. That was a shame. She'd hoped that someday in her immortal life she would be able to see the perfect protectors of the humans be 'drunk' a term she hadn't known of until she'd lived a week in the 21st century. No, they weren't drunk, but they were in sight, which meant that the next step of her plan could be put into action.

Billie closed her eyes and envisioned herself on the beach, the waves and the salty air were present she could feel them. The sand was already finding its way into her boots. It was quiet, and no one was around to hear the conversation she was going to be having in a second. She reached out. Using her magic to connect with the targets until she could see them standing with her. The wind was whipping their hair around there sleeping faces. This was just a dream to them, but they would know that with Billie, all dreams were real in some way or another. Her magic settled, and she felt it all kick into place as if all the wires of a TV were plugged in. Their eyes opened, and Aria and Alice swayed in unison as if they were going to faint. They righted themselves, and their eyes naturally settled on her. She smiled at them. Trying to make it look friendly rather than evil and twisted. Judging from the looks on their faces it was a smile that represented the latter.

"Billie your-"aria said her voice was soft and if Billie wasn't the immortal she was she would've thought that aria was feeling qulity about something. Eddie no doubt. But of course they didn't know she hadn't killed Eddie her best friend. She'll let her live with the quilt a little longer.

"what's going on Billie, where are the others?" Alice cut in, using her questioning voice and rising her eyebrows, trying to be outspoken and demanding. Billie liked her.

" I would like too apologise" Billie started. Trying to remember the speech she'd recited to herself in the mirror earlier that day. " ive come here in a peaceful way In the hopes to make you a deal"

"what kind of deal?" aria said, her voice more defined now she'd gotton over the shock.

"I want to help you, I don't expect you to want to trust me" billie was eyeing them, trying to make out their answers before they said them. She'd been around along time and this was something she was an expert at. So billie knew they were going to bite the bait.

" you're right, she killed Eddie and you want to help us?" alice said pointing a gloved finger at aria. Her eyes were scanning Billie's face and she guessed she was doing the same thing to her.

" yes" billie replied, taking a stet forwards into the sand so that she was more than 2 metres away from them. " all the criminals, ill get rid of them by tomorrow"

" and what can we do f or you?"aria said her voice just as stern as her face. They were trying not to be delighted at the idea. Their biggest issue right now could be solved for them in a matter of seconds, they were trying not to seem to keen.

" help me destroy The end of the world" Billie announced, her words seeming to drown out all the wind and noise around them. The look on the girls faces was the best thing she'd seen in a while.

" and why would you want to do that? " Alice asked, crossing her arms. She was trying to see a hole in the deal. After all Billie was offering them two things that they wanted. The criminals gone and the end of the world destroyed.

" as you can imagine, working with three boys is a challenge"

Both of them looked at her astonished." you want to destroy the end of the world because the boys you work with are a *challenge*?" aria said stepping towards Billie. "You expect us to believe that?"

" I don't expect you to believe me, I expect you to take the offer, I want the chance to go it alone and being tied down by malus, spiral and carligo isn't how I'm going to do it. Being lovey strong women yourselves I would assume you know what that feels like."

"how do we know you won't just turn on us and kill us all?"

Billie was happy that they were asking these questions. They weren't hard to answer and regardless of the answer they all knew they were going to make the deal. They were desperate, the avid drinking and dancing proved it. Eddie was no doubt causing them a disruption and if they still believed he was felix then they were looking for answers. And answers they were going to get if they took the deal. She saw all this occur in their heads while waiting for her response so she took her hand out of her coat pocket and held it out in front of her. It took a few seconds before Alice brought her hand out in a handshake none of them committed too.

"Too put it simply" billie said as she let go of Aria's hand and winking at her ", you don't"

CHAPTER 10
IF YOU WANT SOMETHING DONE...

Malus Lerve was powerful, strong, and apparently unable to control his team. Billie had disappeared while out looking for Eddie, Eddie was doing his best to not be found and to make matters worse Carligo Bellator and spiral James were out on a pub crawl. Without him.

Their underground base was supposed to be a place of evil and demise but all it reeked of lately was cheap whiskey and desperation. Malus didn't like it. They'd left the world how they wanted it and now it seemed they weren't moving forwards. The time was coming for the next step of their plan to fall into place and for it too all work out they were relying on Eddie and his state of mind. Malus was prepared, he knew a lot about time travel and so did spiral James, they of course didn't want to talk to much about it to the others as information is power.

Malus knew that even though Eddie had been in the future for just a few minutes theoretically, time travel bends time and that few minutes could've easily been months or even years for Eddie. Months or years for Eddie to enviably change who he is or was. It was interesting also as Eddie knew what was going to happen to them all if he had been many years into the future, that was the only advantage he saw them having. A way to know what was going to happen before anyone else did, malus just hoped with all the evil in his heart that he hadn't told anyone else about it. Even if he was just in the future for a few minutes, those minutes in the future were more valuable to malus and the rest of the end of the world now more than ever.

Malus needed Eddie back as soon as possible and it looked to him that whatever billie was doing instead of that, it wasn't getting anything done quickly and so Malus thought grabbing his gun from the small table by the door, If he wanted Eddie back and spilling information, he would have to do it himself.

※　※　※

Aria wasn't too keen on the immortal escorting them back to the academy like a angry mum dragging her daughters away from the club after grounding them. Billie was escorting them because she knew where the criminals were and avoiding them right now was their main focus. Getting back to the academy was the only thing Aria could even think about doing. She didn't want to think about the new information she'd learnt and she sure as hell didn't want to think about the deal they'd just made with an immortal evil villain who, aria had noticed didn't seem to get cold despite her lack of clothing.

Billie wasn't saying anything and aria had guessed that she hadn't spent more than half an hour with anyone like them. Or anyone who wasn't like her before. She could sense that she was on edge, nervous about something.

The what, Aria was determined to find out. She didn't trust Billie to deliver the promises she'd made them and both aria and Alice were anxious to find out what Billie actually had in store for them.

The academy was bleak and the almost festive vibe of it three hours ago had disappeared, everyone had either gone out on patrol again or gone to bed destined to have heavy hangovers too look forward too. Aria was glad no one was around to see who they were brining into their safe space. Into their home. If they knew that a member of the end of the world was sleeping in the same building as them tonight, she didn't think her and Alice would be trusted to even cook the academy's meals let alone run it.

It did help though to know that Felix was back, in whatever state or form he was in he still provided a comfort aria didn't know she needed, he was someone who she knew would understand her and Alice's reasons for making the deal with Billie despite the risks it carried.

The lift up to the 5th floor where the bedrooms were, was the only point in their commute where Billie actually spoke. It was more of a murmur under her breath but both Alice and aria heard the words.

"Blood type"

Alice was frowning as she looked over at aria, aria shrugged and Alice brought her index fingers up and moved them in circler motions around her head, indicating that she thought Billie had gone nuts. Aria smiled, and nodded in agreement although she suspected that Billie had properly been nuts since she was born. What she had meant by 'blood type' aria didn't know but it didn't sound like the beginnings of a murderous plot against her or anyone else at the academy so she didn't question it.

When the elevator dinged and the doors opened onto the long red walled hallway that had hundreds of bedrooms branching off of it, Billie stepped out first a hesitant front in her steps that suggested that she wasn't sure where she was supposed to go from there. Aria and Alice followed, flanking Billie on her left and right.

They walked the hallway in silence and the amount of tension in the air wasn't clean cut or even suffocating it was more of a light sweat that was on all of their brows. Nothing like this had happened before. The enemy had never offered up the chance to solve all there problems for seemingly the same goal. Aria was looking at this from the outside, as she suspected Declan and Luke would look at it when they came back. They would see Billie, a member of the end of the world. A person who killed her father Jason Creed. A person who is meant to be a part of the force her herself fight against in the prophecy to save the world. She didn't think they or anyone looking into this situation would take it well. Both She and Alice were crazy. Completely insane. And she guesses that's what being in charge does to you.

When they'd finally gotten to the door that utermatly led to Felix's room, Billie stopped sharply and turned to face her and Alice.

"Ladies first" she said stepping aside too let aria open the door. Aria just smiled and reached over to turn the handle, not moving to step in front of Billie. She wasn't stupid.

The door swung open and aria motioned for Billie to step in before her. Billie did so and they all marched into Felix's room without the full knowledge that he was going to be in there.

CHAPTER 11
BILLIE

Eddie had thought it had been dream. He couldn't lie sometimes his dreams had felt so real that it took until he actually woke up too realize his brain had just made up a complete scenario in his head.

So he was surprised to find that when he'd woken up from his nap, he was in Felix's bed in the academy and eight years into the past. Where he belonged. The wind was howling outside and the violent drumming of rain on his window was the thing that drew his attention to the desk placed just under the windowsill about two metres from his bed. The desk itself was black and covered in papers and books that the actual Felix had put out pursumerly sometime before he'd left the room for good. As he looked he could feel the hairs on his arms and on his neck stand up and he sat up to look closer.

Lying next to a heavily bound book that was placed just off centre, was a single cup of blood. He knew it was blood because the first thing that'd washed over him as soon as he'd seen it was the smell. It smelt of metal and old fruit. He gagged and got sheepishly to his feet. The room was still dark and the only light in the room was coming from the lamp on the desk only a few centimetres from the cup. It was still night outside too which meant he hadn't been asleep for long and that cup of blood had defiantly not been there before he'd come in meaning that whoever had put it there for whatever reason had come in while he'd been asleep. Goosebumps washed over him and he sank back onto the bed, not quite sure what to do and if, the cup of blood aside, he should be worried.

The blood seemed to him like a warning, like someone was telling him to be careful or worse that something was going to happen to him. Eddie could only think of a select group of immortals who want that for him but, he thought, pulling a hoodie over his head, that would only be the case if they knew.

He breathed in and shook his head to himself. They couldn't know what he was thinking, if they were stalking him they'd see him here and surely assume he was being undercover before they'd think of him ever turning good. Yes that was right, he smiled, the anxious pit in his stomach closing up. If that was the case, who had left him this cup of blood and what was the intention? To scare him? To leave a message, yes but what could a cup of blood possibly tell someone?

Eddie stood, streaching his arms and legs and rubbing his eyes. This was something he'd had to learn to do after a few weeks of being completely human. Immortality had given him life easy and within weeks of being normal he'd had to learn when to eat, when to drink everything was new to him, even the sensation of needing the toilet was odd. He liked it though, it gave him things to do where normally back in his immortal life he'd resorted to killing to keep himself busy.

Now he was stood, he could see the contents of the desk more clearly in the lamp light and something caught his eye once again. A note left underneath the cup. The pit that was slowly closing in his stomach was ripped open again and his mouth went dry.

So this was the message the blood was supposed to have given him. He didn't want to take the three steps it took to walk over to the desk and read it. He didn't want too but something inside him made his legs work.

His hands were shaking slightly as he reached down to take the cup of blood off the white envelope that appeared underneath it. There wasn't a name on the front so it wasn't addressed to him but the premise of leaving it in his room was enough too spur on his hands to reach in and take out the folded piece of paper inside.

The writing was joined and the –

The door opened behind him and Eddie whirled dropping the letter back on the desk behind him and moving over to cover the sight of the cup filled with blood. Aria was stood In the door way next to two others. he saw brown hair and the slight tip of a dagger and guessed the person on the left was alice although it was hard to see in the lamp light. His eyes were still tired from sleep so it took him a minute to see the red boots, the pale ivory skin and the blue short hair of Billie.

Eddie took in a sharp breath. Her eyes were trained on him like a dog. Those red, infernal irises locked on to him like a falon ready to swoop down for the kill. Even with her eyes that looked like fire dancing in the centre of them, Billie still managed to make the gaze they held him with icy and cold. He almost felt like shivering.

Eddie hadn't realised that Aria had been speaking to him and he quickly snapped up his head to look as her warm brown eyes that seemed to brighten in the glow of the lamp light. She was staring at him, waiting for him to answer a question he hadn't heard.

Eddie cleared his throat and aria fronwed at the sudden awkwardness of the situation. " sorry did we wake you?" she asked him then.

" Aria, why is she here" eddie managed to croak out, there was a lump in his throat and the intense stare billie was looking at him with was causing his hands to shake.

Aria looked over at alice who was staring behind him at the desk, clearly she'd seen him drop the note behind him as soon as they came in. she didn't voice her curiosity though as aria stepped forward so she was standing just in front of billie, like she was protecting her.

" she's going to help us"

Eddie almost couldn't believe aria's words. He'd known billie for most of her life and he knew more than anyone in that room that billie was going to do everything but help them. Billie was still looking at him, she was trying to sus him out and the fact that he looked visibly older didn't seem to be fazing her, or if it was she wasn't showing it.

" Billie. Billie is going to help you? why? What did she say?" eddie said, his mind finally being able to process billie and her presence here as something that was a bad thing for his cover.

"'she' can speak for herself" Billie said. Hearing her voice for the first time since he'd seen her last was weirder than he'd expected it to be. The last time he'd heard her speak had been her death where she screamed eddies name as the insane-

-He didn't want to think about that. Instead he focused on trying not to throw up the alohol he'd consumed a few hours earlier and the dozen or so cocktail sausages he'd found a new love for while attending the party that celebrated his return. Now though he didn't feel like celebrating, the presence of billie in the room made him want to go back, wish he'd never returned in the first place.

Of course billie can't know what he was thinking, that he had fallen in love with this place, this magic. She couldn't know it and she wouldn't. he needed to act like a villain pretending to be a fake good guy with also actually being a good guy. And they said being undercover wasn't hard. In his head he was only undercover for Billie, he had to pretend to be like the old eddie, the eddie that would've killed everyone at the academy already.

" I am going to help them get rid of the criminals still roaming the streets." Billie said, her voice cold and stern. Saying it like it was a fact and not a promise. Eddie frowned, not having to pretend that his confusion was real.

" why? You're the one who put them there in the first place. You must want something in return right? So what is it?" eddie's words came out at the speed of bullets firing out of a gun. He had to stop himself from shouting, his adrenaline was pumping and by the way Alice and aria were looking at him, they'd expected him to take this encounter better.

Billie just smiled at him. She was either impressed with

his 'acting' skills or legitimately laughing at him. He didn't think she expected this from him either, felix or not. Eddie was starting to loose track of who he was supposed to be in this situation. Alice and aria knew he'd changed so surely they weren't expecting a standard felix Quinn reaction and surely billie would've known that to be here he was having to play a part in some shape or form. Just not the part she thought he was playing.

" yes. Felix. In return, they, you and the rest of the academy are going to help me destroy the rest of the end of the world" Billie was looking at him when she said this, really looking at him because she was waiting for his 'Eddie' reaction. The reaction that a former member of the end of the world would give to the news of an betrayal being so casually announced. Eddie was surprised, shocked even. He hadn't expected that from Billie. Billie the women who treated that group like it was her reason for living. If she left it or even destroyed it what would happen to her? What would happen to the rest of them?

Eddie swallowed, searching the faces of the three girls before him and only finding them to be stern and anxious for him to say something. When finally he did his voice came out in a whisper and his it broke half way.

"How do you intend to uh- " he paused. A lump had formed in his throat.

"Destroy" Billie cut in.

"The end of the world? Aren't they like your mates or something?"

Billie smiled but there was sadness in her eyes that only he could see because he was the only one who was facing her. "You know the prophecy. The only way to destroy the end of the world is to..."

"find the four evolvers" he answered, his voice still quiet. He couldn't quite look at her and the floor was much less intimidating so he rested his eyes on the pile of socks and underwear in the middle of the floor.

"And you already have two of them, so I'm going to help you find the rest."

Even aria and Alice were shocked at this and started talking at the same time. Eddie was glad for their input because it took the pressure of him to say the right things in return.

" if we knew how to find them, billie, don't you think we would've rounded them all up by now" alice said, proberly with more force and attitude than anyone would ever dare use to speak to billie.

" that's because you don't have an immortal friend who can make a device that can find evolvers" billie replied, cool, calm and collected.

There was another round of silence from eddie, aria and alice.

" you – your getting spiral James to help-" Eddie started.

"help build a device that will help find evolvers and in turn help destroy the very group he's apart of," billie said, she took a breath " yes"

" isn't that-" alice began

" kind of messed up" aria finished.

" have you never met me?" billie said, smiling wickedly again " anyway he's already made the device, we just have to steal it"

" we?" eddie asked. Another flurry of anxiety swarming him. If he was meant to go into the end of the worlds base then they would expect him to return or still be the same eddie.

Billie was already turning to leave through the doorway, her dark red eyes still mannging to glow in the shadows of his room. Aria and alice were quick to resume there defensive postions, still not pursadued enough to trust billie and let her roam the acamdey by herself.

" ever heard of a getaway car?" she said fading into the dark hallway beyond. Eddie watched as alice followed. Aria turned to leave too but when she got too the doorway she stopped and turned to look at him.

" I think now would be a good time to read the note" she said. Looking behind him at the table and the cup of blood on it. She smiled slightly and left him alone in the room.

Eddie turned rapidly, stopping himself from running after her and asking her what it all meant. If she knew what the note said could that mean that she was the one who wrote it?

He took the piece of paper off the desk and sat down on his bed to read it.

CHAPTER 12
MORE THAN ONE

L uke wasn't sure how being undercover worked but the risk he was taking showing off his skills as care free as he was in the training sessions he had started to attend in his mission to scout out Ryan. He couldn't help but be faster, be stronger than the other boys. The feeling of using all the elements give him and not having to get hit or struck with weapons in doing so was liberating, he was finding that he was having fun.

Ryan, not so much. He was so obviously trying not to show off and that was causing him problems with the rest of the boys. Luke was on the same side as him in most practises and was trying to give him the space to perform and show what magic was in his blood. Ryan was doing the opposite and seemed to have his walls up after their previous conversation, they hadn't spoken but Ryan looked at him as if he'd gone and burnt all his kit in the locker room. Ryan was trying to hide something from everyone and Luke knew what it was and this wasn't sitting well with Ryan but it was sitting very well with Luke. Very well indeed.

Jason had always trained them that emotions were always an asset to you especially when using the elements. Whatever Ryan was feeling sooner or later it was going to fuse into something he couldn't control and that would be when the real Ryan came out, Luke just needed to make sure they were alone when that happened.

Practice was over and Luke was pretty sure that would be the last one he would be attending. He needed to get home and he needed Ryan to come with him, first through he needed to talk to Declan, tell him everything before he attempted to 'kidnap' him for terms of a better word. Declan would tell him he was stupid but that was nothing new. Luke was also excited to see what Declan had been doing and if he had found anything that would help them.

He was walking down a quiet road, the heat of the day gone with the daylight and now the moon was high above him, he breathed in the cool air and wrapped his jacket tighter around him. He felt different, like every nerve of his was on fire. Yet the cooling impact of the air around him seemed to penetrate his skin and reach deep into his veins. He wasn't sure what was causing it but he was sure it had something to do with the fact that he'd felt different ever since the day, the moment, the very second where he opened his eyes again after fearing he'd never opened them again after being in the ecploasion that had killed him.

It couldn't explain it but the magic he had in him felt off like the seat of a car being in the wrong place after you've let somebody else drive. He was the same luke, the same boy just a different ora surrounded him and now suddenly it was starting to take a form. This burning, this confliction in feelings was something he'd never felt but he had seen it before in Aria shortly after her ritual. It had lead her to lose control and simualtiously killed Eddie.

He didn't want that, if this was the same thing, if somehow he was going through the after effects of the evolver ritual without actually bring one.

He had to get his mind of this and back to the matter at hand. He took put his phone and with quick tenitive hands he dillaied Declan's number. He picked up on the third ring and Luke, ignoring all small talk got straight down to the facts.

"Declan, I think I have one" Luke said down the speaker, a little too aggressively than he would like. "I think he could be an evolver, he's a basketball player, he's massive, fast basically –"

"Luke" Declan's voice sharply tried to intercept him at the other end.

"- me but not obvs not as" Luke continued, not paying attention.

"Luke"

"cool, good-looking"

"LUKE" Declan suddenly shouted making Luke jump violently.

"What?"

"I've found *them*" Declan said, his voice back to its former calm volume.

"Them? You mean –"

"More than one *yes*"

There was a second of silence as Luke took in this information. It was exactly what he wanted to hear. "That's so good Declan. What do we do now?"

"im bringing them home, you try and get yours back

there too"

" I was just ringing to confirm that kidnapping is okay to do"

" luke you know Im not your dad right?"

" I know but you are my companion on this mission"

"Luke your smart do whatever it takes, I'll see you on the other side"

"See you there" he paused, a smile snaked onto his lips " dad"

CHAPTER 13
UNLUCKY

S piral James was not having a good week. Somehow he kept getting things wrong, and that was worrying not because he was never wrong but because he couldn't be wrong. Especially when it came to building something that has never been made before. It was his magic, his unique trait that no one else processed. So why, this week of all weeks had he failed to build a machine that could go back in time. It was meant to be his significant creation, his big chance to show Malus that he was the best member of the end of the world. But now he was out, wandering the streets that he'd partaken in making empty. The ten beers he'd consumed with carligo earlier that night had had more effect on him than he'd thought possible.

In fact, he was pretty sure he was starting to see things. Well one thing, one person. The figure of Felix Quinn running towards him. In the darkness, he wasn't sure if it was the trick of the street light above him or how he was walking, slightly to the left of the road, but he could see that this vision of Felix running full pelt towards him was frantic, tears streaming down his face.

Spiral closed his eyes and stopped walking. When he opened them again, the vision of Felix was still there, but it had gotten closer, so now it was at least ten metres away. He squinted his eyes trying to make sure he was actually seeing what he was seeing because if it was Felix Quinn then Eddie had come back from where spiral had sent him and if that was the case then he knew precisely where Billie was. The Felix that was running towards him looked evidently older than the last time he'd seen him, and for that to happen in the two days, it had been since spiral had sent him there then Malus and his fears of the trip to the future being longer than they'd thought, were well and truly real.

The night was hiding him in the shadows so the figure of Felix hadn't seen him yet and spiral didn't know if he should expose himself to his gaze and let him know he was there. After all, Malus did want Eddie back and getting him back for there leader would defiantly get spiral back into his good books.

He was about to step forwards out of the shadows when a voice tailing Eddie, called after him. It was a girls voice. High pitched and tinged with worry.

"Felix? Where are you going?" aria creed said, stepping into the light made from one of the lamp posts nearby. She was drenched in sweat, and mud was splattered over her black attire. Her hair as red as it was plastered to her skull, the little strands that were sticking up were wind-blown and knotted. It was clear to spiral that she had been in some sort of fight to get here. Eddie had changed pace, so he was walking now, his eyes still fixed on the path in front. He walked past where spiral was hiding in the shadows, and it took everything in his power not to reach out and grab him. He wanted to see how this played out.

"Felix, please stop." Aria had stopped running and was stood looking at the back of Felix's head. Even from here, spiral could see the frustration in her eyes. Her fingers were moving slightly, and the wind was starting to pick up. The leaves on the ground around his feet were whipping into the air, and as if a car had slammed into his body, Felix jerked backwards, flying through the air before he hit the ground at Aria's feet.

She was looking at him, annoyed and spiral couldn't help but snigger. Malus was going to love hearing about this. Felix was groaning as he got to his feet. "what?" he asked out of breath, clearly winded by the impact.

Aria just laughed more in agitation than anything else. "Felix, I do not have time for this. You cannot treat people like – like there-"

"like there different. Like they don't belong?" Felix said. His voice was strained like he was upset. Spiral shook his head, this was like watching a tv drama. Better than watching Malus explode things with his mind.

"because that's how I feel Aria. Ever since I've got back, you've been acting differently around me. Everyone has been."

Aria looked stunned at his comment and just shook her head in disbelief. "what? Felix, you went to the future, you lived there for five years. You've changed, of course, were going to act differently around you." There was a pause before Aria spoke again, "Is this about luke?"

Eddie scoffed. "why does everything have to be about luke?" his voice was raised now, and spiral was impressed as he'd never heard Eddie raise his voice to anyone. "I may have been gone, but that doesn't change the fact that it was only three months for you. Three months and three months compared to five years is nothing." His arms were flailing everywhere, and spiral guessed they were trying to help Eddie make a point.

"what are you talking about? Felix how can you expect me to act normally at all when you come back from the future... something I didn't even know could actually happen until you popped out of nowhere, you came back and told me that I died in your arms. How can you think that wouldn't affect me? And then- the insane? The end of the end getting destroyed? The human race getting killed? Tell me, Felix, how am I supposed to act knowing that all this stuff, this horrible unthinkable stuff is going to happen?" there were tears in her eyes, and as far as spiral can see, she hadn't let any fall.

Eddie was shaking his head like he was trying to get something out of it. He signed, and when he spoke again, his voice was even and stern.

"none of that has changed me, Aria. Not like this. Sure I've seen some things I'd rather not see but hasn't changed me."

Spiral was shocked to find that he was holding his breath so he could hear every word of his speech to Aria. This was all new information to him, the things Aria had said Eddie had told her were going to happen in the future were only just sinking in, and he didn't know entirely what they meant. The end of the world being destroyed. That was what Aria had said. He shivered at the thought of it, the idea of losing was almost hurtful.

The insane was another thing he was eager to find out more about, he'd never heard of such words and to have it said so casually by Aria just concluded to spiral that Eddie was telling them things before he was telling them.

He brought his attention back to Eddie and Aria.

"Aria "Eddie was saying, "what im trying to say is- what you don't understand is that the world is going to change so quickly and so suddenly in the next few years and-"he broke off. His voice catching on a word he couldn't quite get out.

"– I know how fast it can go. Hell, we are not prepared for it." He had stepped closer to Aria and spiral could sense they were about to makeup and all would be fine in the world. Despite the fact he wanted to find out more, find out more about what the future holds, spiral needed to get the information he already knew back to the rest of the end of the world before he was seen here.

He turned and quietly suttled along the fence he'd been hidden by and rounded the corner into the night.

❄ ❄ ❄

Aria looked at Felix. Her hands were shaking, and her heart was a pulsating mess in her chest.

"do you think it worked? Do you think it was enough?" even though she was addressing him, she couldn't look Felix in the eyes. Not yet.

"Yeah. He was gone." Felix said in a sigh, he wasn't looking at her either. They stood there the two of them, only a few seconds past, but it felt like hours. Hours of them sitting in this awkwardness.

Aria turned to go, but Felix was there and grabbed her

arm to stop her. "wait, im not done."

When Aria looked at him again, he was looking at her, something careful and precise glinting in his eyes.

She laughed nervously, confused that he was still playing along to the plan even with spiral james gone. "what? You don't have to say anymore he's gone, he's –"

Felix put his hands up, stopping her mid-sentence. "I wasn't just saying that stuff for him, I was saying it for me. For you"

Aria closed her eyes, not too sure if she was doing it so she couldn't see the look on his face, which was that of a puppy. Longing for forgiveness for something he had not yet done, or because she was trying to focus on what he had actually said, now that it mattered.

"so you actually meant everything you were saying?" she said once she'd reopened her eyes, her voice only slightly hysterical.

He was still looking at her, and without removing his gaze from hers, he paused and then as smoothly as if he was saying her name, he said "yes."

She flinched like she'd been slapped and she couldn't help feeling hurt by it. When she didn't respond, he continued. "aria, you know something's different about me but have you ever thought that maybe the reason why I am different is because im just not the same person anymore."

"But you just said none of that stuff in the future changed you."

"it didn't."

"yes, I think it did, Felix. Everything about you is different." She stepped closer so that they were only a few centimetres apart. She looked into his eyes. Saw the same gorgeous blue in them but she also saw the tiny patch of red that was and had been growing and mixing in with the eyes original colour for days now. A glint of purple was present in the space they had mixed, and Aria couldn't help but feel sick looking at it.

"you look different. You talk differently. You act different, god Felix, even your eyes are different." She turned so that her back was to him. She could sense that he was stood frozen behind her. "what can I do Felix but suspect that you are different" she said in a voice so small she didn't know If he'd heard it.

Her body tensed when he put his hand on her shoulder, his sudden warmth was soothing, and she felt her body relax as he spoke.

"Aria, I do not deny that, but please just listen to me. The events, the things that happened then in the future didn't change me. You did. The person you are in eight years did. Aria Creed changed me."

She whipped round to face him again, her thoughts jumbling into one. "what?" she whispered. Trying to pluck the answer, his except experiences and thoughts from the place she saw them in his eyes. He was about to answer when her phone rang, making her jump.

She fumbled in her pockets and looked at her the screen. She gasped as she read the name starting back at her, she looked at Felix who had looked once at the screen and given up on the rest of the conversation.

Butterflies leapt in her stomach, and a slick, animated smile slid onto her face. Without waiting for another second, she tapped and answered the call, turning away from Felix as the soft velvety voice of Luke Quinn spoke through the speaker.

CHAPTER 14
BACK TOGETHER

"**L**uke, you're alive" Aria's voice rang through the speakers, to Luke's relief, she seemed happier to hear from him and not like she hated his guts.

"No, I'm calling from beyond the grave," he said, trying to be not so sarcastic that she remembered why she should be annoyed with him.

"You might as well be," Aria remarked, her voice starting to creep into the zone of 'annoyed.'

"What is that supposed to mean?" he said, again trying to keep his tone light.

"You didn't tell anyone where you were or what you were doing" boom. There it was, the zone of which he didn't want this conversation to be in. She was now annoyed.

"that's the point of being undercover," he said, his palms had started to sweat, and he couldn't even blame the Texan sun for that as it had disappeared over the horizon hours ago.

"Undercover? But you weren't –"

"– Declan put me undercover in a high school," Luke interjected before she could accuse him of lying.

There was a sudden fit of laughter from the other end of the receiver and Luke despite being glad that she was laughing at him instead of shouting at him, had to pull the phone away from his ear.

"I've been to school luke, and there is no way you stayed undercover, and god forbid unnoticed," she said, all annoyed tones went from her voice.

"you could say that, but I've found someone, someone who could be an evolver, one of yours."

"no way really?" her voice picked up, and he could tell that she was smiling.

"yes, his name is Ryan, "he said, turning his voice into a whisper like he was afraid anyone around him would hear the name.

"well, Luke we have some pretty good news too but – I think I should wait until your back before I tell you." Aria's voice had turned almost shaky, and Luke didn't wasn't to press it in fear that it was news he didn't want to hear.

"I won't be home for a few days yet, I've gotta find a way to –"

"kidnap," she said flatly.

"yes, kidnap Ryan."

Luke hung up the phone, acutely aware that he hadn't said any parting words to her, he didn't want to talk to her over the phone, he didn't want to talk to anyone over the phone. Those conversations were always the worst because they were the conversations that hurt the most, they substituted the person's presence with just there voice, and he hated it. Someone's voice couldn't tell you anything, someone's face, however, could tell you a thousand things with one shift of a movement.

The road down to the house him and Declan had brought was stony and uneven, and he ran down it, rocking from side to side. The door handles of the front door were always stiff, and it creaked as it opened. A sound Luke always associated with horror movies.

He stepped into the hallway which always smelt of dust and old wood regardless of the amount of times he'd sprayed it with lynx Africa. The lights were already on, and the low, warm glow of them burned as his eyes adjusted from the hash darkness of the night outside. Luke was about to head to the kitchen, which lay through the door in front of him, in the middle of the two sets of stairs that led up to the second floor when someone cleared their throat behind him.

* * *

Billie was in the 'waiting room', which she guessed was just a posh way of saying outside the room you are meant to be in. The chair she was sat on wasn't comfy, and she supposed that they weren't meant to be so that you'd be happy to leave them what you eventually get called to do so. The meeting room Aria and Alice were in was in front of her, its doors were shut of course, and their thick oak doors were plastered in symbols of earth, water, fire and air.

She had her legs crossed because she thought she looked kinder that way. Billie was bored. She had been so excited by her current events and big decisions that she had forgotten to make sure she had some fun left for times like these. She had successfully made the academy a deal, she had successfully found Eddie, post future, and most importantly she had found a way to be left alone in this place without someone looking over her shoulder. It was progress.

Aria and Alice were discussing Billie's place here, it was stupid because Billie knew they didn't trust her, but they so badly needed her help. No discussion was required really, but humans did need to talk about things to make them feel like they found the best solution.

There was a sound from behind her, down the hall. She didn't turn to see who it was because she already knew. Eddie rounded the corner, his now stalk black hair swinging with him as he walked over to a chair just a few over from Billie and sat. He said nothing.

Billie turned in her seat to look at him. Study him closer up. The blue of his eyes was magnified by the light flooding in through the window next to him. After a few seconds, she heard him suck in a breath.

"Billie,," he said, his voice wasn't accusing, it was more acknowledging.

"Eddie," she said back, coping his tone of voice and trying to catch his eye's gaze.

"you found me quicker than I thought you would, I am glad to see you, but you've got to know something before I come with you" he wasn't looking at her and despite being mildly frustrated at this, Billie couldn't help but sense a sadness about him that was all too familiar.

"fine, but what makes you think im not staying?" she asked him. Curious. He didn't answer, and she let that thought sink in, maybe he had thought that Billie had come to take him back, but she couldn't help but wonder if he wanted that at all, to return to them. After a while, Eddie spoke again.

"spirals machine, it – "

"Took you to the future, yes I got that," she said, indicating his new grown-up face and frankly all-new body. It was weird to see him like this, like a shell, almost like an armour. Eddie's immortal body was perfect and even seeing Eddie, hearing Eddie with the face of a human, magic or not was something quite fascinating. The fact that the body he was using was Felix's made it even stranger, a boy she couldn't help but favour. She wasn't sad that now that boy was gone, she couldn't be, but she was regretful that he had been the one Eddie had chosen to swap with. Afterall if Aria were gone, the prophecy could not take place.

"Not just into the future" Eddie was saying, his voice almost sounded hurt by her casual dismissal, "years into it where I've lived there for five years, Billie."

Eddie looked at her then. Right in the eyes. What she had thought she had felt coming off him as sadness was magnified in his eyes. Such anguish was flooded in them that Billie had to fight the unpronounced urge to look away. A knot had formed in her stomach, and for some reason, she felt like she couldn't respond. Eddie had been left in the future for five years. In that time, anything could've happened, and she knew a lot had.

"But it's only been two days," she said finally, her voice still strong but she couldn't help the little flutter of surprise waver her words.

"Maybe for you but I've lived a different life, the things

I've seen –" he broke off, and Billie could see he was playing quite franticly with the hem of his blue jumper.

"What things have you seen? " she asked, slowly "does the end of the world.." she trailed off not wanting to finish the question because she knew the answer could be shocking.

Eddie just paused a moment and shifted on his chair slightly. "– the end of the world comes but not at the hands of us."

Billie was glad to hear that he still used the term 'us', she swallowed even though she didn't need too, that wasn't the answer she'd expected, but it did hold hope in it "What then, how?"

The doors to the meeting room opened suddenly, and Aria's head popped out, her eyes flicking between both Billie and Eddie, a question in them that she didn't voice as she indicated with her hand that Billie should stand.

"Billie was ready to see you now."

❉ ❉ ❉

"so Billie, you suddenly want to help us" Alice was saying as Aria, crossed the room to stand beside her. Billie was standing, her body resting against the left wall. Despite the twenty-odd chairs encircling the large, long rectangular table in the middle of the room, none of them was seated.

"and we don't trust you to do that" Aria said, leading on from Alice's sentence.

Billie nodded once, "you'd be stupid if you did."

"glad we've got that cleared up." Alice said, nodding back

to her. "did you get the device?" she asked after a few seconds. There was a sort of electricity in her voice that Aria thought reminded her of a live wire. Of course, this device could change everything. It meant they would be able to find the final three evolvers, the people at the academy have been waiting for that to happen for decades and Alice since she was little. There were stars in her eyes as Billie reached into her pocket and pulled out a small black box. Aira had to stop herself from running over and grabbing it from her, and she could sense that Alice was doing the same.

Billie stepped forward and placed it in the centre of the table. When she stepped back, she smiled.

"so the distraction worked then?" Alice asked Aria, she nodded, not wanting to think about what had happened on that road and especially didn't want to think about spiral james being the one to witness it.

"and we finally heard from luke, he said he's found a potential evolver and that hes coming home in a few days," Aria said, staring at the faint black lines on the box intently. They were engraved in small patterns all over the outside of it, and something about the box was captivating her. She couldn't concentrate, and Alice had to nudge her with her elbow before Aria could turn to face her.

"uh sorry, the box- I think it's like calling me or something."

Billie chuckled "well it is used for finding evolvers, the fact that you're this close to it will be a little detracting."

"so spiral built this?" Alice asked, not hiding the fact that she was impressed.

"How does it work?" Aria asked quickly, she was suddenly

itching to get things moving, and as it happened, things weren't moving fast enough.

"ask it," Billie said, motioning to the box with a gloved hand.

"ask it what?" Alice demanded. Her face was pulled into a scowl, and only Aria knew that was the face of someone who wasn't going to laugh at being made to feel stupid.

Billie sighed. "matchbox." She said. The box on the table started to glow faintly a dull but solid red shined from its corners. Aria gasped and couldn't help but lean forwards, Alice did the same beside her, and they watched as Billie stepped forwards and asked it point blankly.

"where are the remaining three evolvers that partake in full filling the prophecy?" after she had finished speaking, the light went out, and the body of the box started shifting. It opened in half so now it was a rectangle and an inverted image was displayed on it. White outlines illustrated buildings and trees, and as Billie leaned forwards to expand the image it projected outwards with her fingers, Aria could see that it was a map.

Four bright red dots were visible against the blackness of the screen and Aria drew in a sharp breath when she realised what they represented. The four evolvers.

Billie moved the map again, zooming in on one of the dots. "this is you" she said, "see the academy, and this is the room we are currently in"

She did see, saw the dot that represented her and the white lines of the walls that currently surrounded it. Her heart was thundering in her chest, and she swallowed hard before turning to Alice, who had gone pale, and hugged her.

"the matchbox will show you the location of the dots in order, so the dot furthest away will be the last one you visit" Billie's voice was muffled as Aria's body was crushed by Alice's, it was like she was trying to squeeze all the past few months stress and anxiety they had felt together, out in one hug.

"visit?" Aria questioned, pulling away from Alice.

"for the dot to fade, the person representing the dot has to touch the box in some way so – "she took the box in-between her gloved fingers and walked around the table, so she was only a metre from where Aria stood.

"touch it."

Aria leaned forward and touched the side of the box. It was cold and smooth, but she felt a slight zap of electricity that made her drawback hastily. Alice gasped, and Aria looked as the dot that had once represented her fade from the map.

"now the next dot will come into view, if it's not far away we could probably get the person tonight" Billie was saying.

Aria wasn't listening, her eyes were trained on the map, which was moving slowly over the academy's layout, out into the driveway and just when aira thought it wasn't going to stop, another red dot appeared on the screen.

Before Alice or Billie could say another word. Aria was running for the door.

✱ ✱ ✱

Declan had sunburn. Hot crispy, peeling sunburn. This, combined with the minibus full of equally as sunburnt magical people, wasn't the best cocktail of factors for a four-hour car journey from the airport. The gates to the academy were open, something he'd told both Alice and Aria was a wrong move considering the amount of criminals around. He shook his head as he drove through them and was about to park the van next to the already parked cars in the driveway when Aria, Alice and Brendon all ran out of the front doors and into the path of his vehicle. He slammed the breaks on and stopped about a metre away from Aria. Her hands were out telling him to stop, and for a minute he thought they were warning him of the member of the end of the world, who was at that point walking casually down the stone steps that led up to the academy, but once he'd got the door open he couldn't hear any shouts of protest for him to leave just his name being shouted quite excitedly.

He, however, couldn't be happy that he was home or even glad to see the others because as he had clocked before, Billie was also amongst them. For whatever reason and he was sure Alice and aira had many, but for whatever reason, no one seemed at least bit fazed by the immortal standing almost motionless on the bottom step, and he was about to ask what the hell was going on when Aria grabbed the sleeve of his jacket and pulled him violently out of the truck.

"Aria, what are you-" he started and instantly stopped when he saw another person walk out into the light of the day. He stopped. Everything he saw went in slow motion, and he couldn't get his mind to process the image of Felix Quinn walking past Billie still standing on the steps and running to join Alice and Brendon in watching Aria trying to get Declan out of the truck. As you can imagine, this whole scene wasn't just odd to him, but it was especially bazaar to the people he had waiting in the back.

Once Aria had got him out of the van, she then placed him in front of it, so she was standing in front of him. She then turned and motioned for Billie to come over. Declan tensed, his head was spinning, and If it wasn't for the rain cooling him down he was sure he would've set fire to everything he touched, no one was telling him what was currently taking place. As it stood and from what he could make out from what he could see, the following things had happened while he'd been away.

1. Felix had somehow come back
2. Billie had come back with him
3. Felix had grown – a lot
4. Aria had gotten stronger
5. Alice had cut her hair
6. Nobody had listened to his instructions

"Aria, what the hell is going on. Why is she here, and how is Felix here ?"

Aria just smiled at him. "Declan you're one of them," she said, ignoring his questions.

Billie had come to Aria's side, a device in her hands. Alice was also looking at it, and they all had astonished but not necessarily surprised looks on there faces.

"one of what?" he asked, he could feel himself becoming more and more frustrated with the conversation.

Aria just looked at him, the smile widening into something truly spectacular. "Declan, your one of The four evolvers. One of *my* evolvers."

CHAPTER 15
IN THE EYES, THERE LIES

Eddie was sitting by the window. The sunset was glorious over the horizon and it seemed to light the tree tops in the distance on fire. The clouds seemed to cushion the flames as they tumbled seemingly in slow-motion as the sun disappeared, bringing the night with it.

He was sat at the west wing library gazing absently out the window. It was strange to come back to a world where none of the destruction that he knew was coming had hit yet. He had aria's letter in his hands. The words in it were now memorised in his head and he didn't think he would or could forget them. He wanted to talk to her about it, he wanted to talk to her properly about what he meant when he said that she had changed him. The library right now seemed to be the only place he could get away from the chaos that buzzed around the others. It was hard to be here now that Billie had inserted herself tightly in the centre of that chaos. He knew that no one trusted her but the desperation aria and Alice held in their eyes without even meaning too was enough persuasion for anyone, if they asked why bringing an immortal enemy into the academy was a good idea.

He supposed that he was too an enermy. On paper he wasn't to be trusted either but he couldn't even think about being kicked out of a place he'd felt truly himself. The fact that someday aria and the others would find out who he actually was made his stomach tie itself in knots to think about.

Eddie looked down at his crossed legs that were sat on the window seat in line with the liabry door. He only had socks on his feet and the jumper he was wearing smelt of men's aftershave that wasn't his. His long hair hung in front of his face, he didn't move it away it felt like a shield to him then. All he wanted to do was hide and not come out until everything was over.

This hype, this sudden excitement that had stemmed from Aria declaring Declan as one of the four evolvers that would join her in the battle the prophecy foretold was getting to be too much for him and despite Declan questioning eddie for hours after his arrval, eddie hadn't been much regarded as a person of interest anymore, which in the back of his mind was a good thing as billie hadn't been left alone for more than two mintues since she arrived. He was also aware that if eddie still looked liked eddie, he would have the same treatment.

So he had come to the library to be away from the chaos and to finally think about what he was going to do not only with his fresh start but with billie and her plan to derail the end of the world. He just couldn't believe she would fo it and therefore he knew she had another plan up her sleeve.

Eddie jumped as he heard the double doors of the library creak open. He held his breath somehow hoping that whoever had come in hadn't seen him.

There was a brief silence and Eddie thought he had gotten away with not having to speak to anyone when a voice familiar to him said his name or rather his stolen one.

"Felix" aria said softly, her voice weighed down by something in the way she'd said that name, that slipped away before Eddie could catch it.

He paused before he looked up, bracing himself for what he was going to be looking at. When he did eventually look up at her, aria met his gaze and Eddie couldn't help but want her to say something else.

"Felix" she said agin, her face worried, her eyes sparked. " im sorry for shouting at you"

" aria, you were right" he said, not really knowing what he was saying. " i know that im a new, different person to the one you met three months ago but you have to understand that I –"

" felix, you don't have to explain you just have to realise that I am freaking out" she had stopped walking towards him and was now stood her eyes scanning his face. Her hair was down and it hung long and straight down her back.

" yeah, finding out that Declan Is one of your evolvers is-" eddie started saying, trying to make himself sound calm and not like his heart was beating vionletly in his chest.

" not about that, im freaking out because I don't want to die, felix and I don't want everyone I love to die either" her voice was tinged with worry and her eyebrows were knitted together. Her hands were out like she was waiting for someoe to hug her.

" of course you don't, but I cant tell you I cant –" he said, his voice starting to rise above the calm bracket.

" you cant ? or you wont ?" aria suddenly snapped. Her cheeks had become flushed and eddie had a feeling she might slap him.

" I cant, you said it yourself, I cant tell you"

" do you not trust me?" she said, an acousing air in her voice.

Eddie sighed " of course I trust you, Ive faught beside you for years ive-"

" IM NOT HER" aria screamed at him. Tears had pricked her eyes and she looked away from him, brething heavily.

Eddie couldn't hekp the Silence that bridged the gap between them. He didn't know what to say to her so he just looked at her. At her arms, her legs her face her feet. Looked at her because all he saw was that girl. The firl on the battle field who'd saved his life more times than he wanted to count, that girl who had taught him how to cook in the acmadey's kitchen at 4 am while everyone else was asleep. Aria creed now was just as much the aria creed he'd known in the future.

He closed his eyes, not wanting to see her face as he said his next words.

" yes, you are" he whispered, almost through his teeth.

Eddie heard her suck in a breath " how can I be when she knew what the hell was going to happen to the world and I seem to have no bloody clue how to do anything" aria's voice had gotten calmer and eddie no longer felt loke she was was a threat to him and his slappable face.

" aria, you are powerful, strong and you have time to

learn everything. The first parts of the puzzle are coming together"

" puzzle?" she asked, running her dingers through her hair.

" yeah,like the puzzle of life" he said realzing then how stupid that sounded.

" so the first part of the puzzle is me finding out Declan is one of the four evolvers" she asked impatiently

" I guess" eddie just shugged at her

She went to sit beside him on the window seat, her leather jacket rumperling as she sat. her leg was boucing nervously and her boots were squeaking as she moved.

" so you cant tell me what happens but you can give me clues" her voice was hopfull as she looked at him a sort of delicate wash of relif spead through her features.

" clues? Aria ive told you more than ive should of and as far as clues go the fact that Declan is part of the evolvers should be enough for you"

She stared at him. Her eyes flickering in the low light of dusk. He saw in them a burning curiosity that didn't just brighten her eyes but also seem to set them on fire.

" felix, you said that you don't deny being like a different person." Aira's voice was calm but he tensed that she was fighting back tears. " and you cant tell me more of what the future holds. Luke left a month after you had been taken through that portal." She was talking now like she was reading off a list she had made in her head and eddie couldn't help but notice that the things she was saying all sounded like reasons as to why eddie was a fraud.

" ill say that again," she said once eddie didn't respond. "

luke, your brother, left a month after you had been taken through that portal"

Eddie swore in his head. He knew where this was going. He didn't need to hear the rest of what she was saying. As she spoke he kept his face even, unfazed by her implicit accusation because she didn't need to say it. In her mind, he was felix and to her felix had come back a different person which she could deal with. The felix in her head had come back and slept in his own bed, wore his own clothes eaten at his place at the table but the felix in her mind had seemed to have forgotten, whole heartedly about his own brother.

" you haven't asked about luke once." Aria was saying. She didn't sound angry but he knew it was building. " you didn't even know he was gone"

Eddie swallowed. How could this be the reason get gets caught out. Yes forgetting to care about someone you should be care about was a big mistake on his part but surely aria wasn't going to suspect. Whatever the reason she'd thought of for eddie's uninterest in luke it couldn't be anywhere near the truth of matter. So eddie let go of the breath he only realised then he'd been holding and finally looked into aria's blazing eyes.

❊ ❊ ❊

Now Declan had always thought he was a good fighter. He had also thought he was a good evolver in general. But being classed and named as one of the four evolvers was something that hadn't felt real. Even now with everyone staring at him in the meeting room, he felt odd and floaty like he was in a dream. The seven magical people he'd taken with him from the underground Texan clan were sitting at the table and took up one side of it. They were sipping ineptly at there cups of water and Alice, who was leaning against the wall on the opposite side of the room, was looking at them with amusement in her eyes.

Billie was also leaning against the wall and Declan couldn't help but note that he'd never actually seen Billie sit down before. She was staring into space and everyone had made sure not to stand or sit by her just incase she were to accidently karate chop someone into pieces, or something to that effect.

Brendon and the remaining academy members bordered the room and Declan couldn't help but notice the hole that aria and Felix left when they weren't here. He didn't know if he should say something, Declan supposed that he should as technically with his return he was also was back in charge of the place and to his knowledge there was lots to talk about.

He eyed Alice, who was also looking at him as if to say 'go on then'. He felt like a supply teacher introducing himself to his temporary students, apart from the fact that everyone in this room wasn't likely to throw rulers at him and make him cry.

"First of all, I am happy to be back" Declan said, everyone looked at him then. He coughed " and there is a lot to discuss. I know this is properly the last place you want to be on a Saturday night but please just listen to what I have to say"

" these are some of the representatives from texas." He cast a hand to there side of the table " The others of them will be coming over to the acmadey shortly but they have agreed to help us, this means that they will be living here with us in place of the people we lost at hill view prison." He swallowed. "it has also come to my attention that billie has also agreed to help us"

Nobody said anything and the only thing that moved was Billie's head, which was nodding enthusiastically. " she has agreed to get rid of the criminals and in return she wants our help to destroy the end of the world. Well the rest of them"

He was talking like he was reading the news from a tele-prompter and even he was starting to bore at the sound of his voice. Nobody wanted to hear bad news all the time and by the looks on alice's and brendons faces it looked like that's all they'd been hearing for the past couple of months.

" Declan, aria has it at the moment but " alice began " why don't you tell them of the device"

Declan couldn't see why he should have to tell everyone of the most recent news when he'd just learned of it him-self. He hadn't been around for the past two months he didn't know the ins and outs of what had gone down at the acadmey while he was gone. He wished aria were here because she seemed to know a lot more than alice when it came to describing the events of the past few weeks. He wondered where she was, was she meant to be here? Did she even know this meeting was happening?

" billie, why don't you tell us about it instead, you know more about it than anyone" he said not looking at alice. He heard a few gasps in the crowd and the seven Texans who hadn't taken there eyes off billie since being here, were whispering to each other. It was the tall bald one who spoke now, interrupting billie who had stepped forward from leaning against the wall

" im sorry but how are we even allowing a person like her In here, she's part of the end of the world she cannot be trusted"

" if you would excuse me sir" alice said, her voice only slightly patronising " for someone who lives underground you must not know that the world was overrun with criminals and some are still around totally rendering most of our country a danger zone. We cant get rid of them all and in case you weren't listening, billie here has offered to get rid of them for us" she was staring at the bald man, his features twisted into a cold girmacewhich Declan could only describe as her ' game face'.

" how come theyre still around then? How long has she been here? Gathering information that she can report back to the other immortals" the man was elongating every word and this, Declan could see was getting on alice's nerves.

" im sorry who are you again?" alice asked, she was now leant forwards so that her hands were placed rather rididly on the table. She had a menacing look in her eyes and Declan knew that this was going to result in some sort of idle name calling that he had no doubt alice was going to win.

" Jacob" Jacob said sternly. Alice just smiled.

" well Jacob have you heard of aria creed?"

" yes, she is the third evolver" Jacob said like he was proud of himself for knowing.

" good because she's down stairs"

" right" Jacob just shugged at her.

" now ask billie how many members of the end of the world are left?" alice demanded looking at Jacob with playful intent In her eyes. Declan could see that he hadn't needed to worry about the acadmey being in good hands, alice was very well capable of dealing with things herself.

Jacob spluttered at the tought of actually talking to the immortal he'd critised. They all looked at billie who looked bored, She stared at Jacob with intuitive eyes waiting.

" how many are there left" he managed to croak out.

Billie smiled at him, no sign of sadness in her eyes. " four" she said making mutiple of the people's blood in the room turn cold at just the sound of her voice piercing the air.

More gasps filled the room but only from the remaining six other Texans and alice's eyes shinned as she spoke again. " aria creed killed one of them. By herself."

More gasps erupted and Declan couldn't help but smile at their naivety. It was strnage to him to have other people that knew of the magic that filled there veins, of the power the elements could give them but yet still be so clueless of the events that had shaped their culture.

"so if aria can kill one of them, why can't she kill them all?" a shaggy haired boy who looked about eighteen spoke. He then wished he hadn't.

Alice flickered her gaze to his and Declan could've sworn the boy flinched. " because that would be like asking Poseidon to flood the whole world with water, she would die or at the very least be competely drained afterwards, the only reason she didn't die from killing eddie last time was because –"

She stopped. Her eyes had grown wide and they moved to meet declans. He didn't have to be next to her to see what they had in them. Apart from the sparkle of distant anger and rage, there shinning in the very reaches of her eyes was the raw and unforgiveable image of realisation.

CHAPTER 16
THE SECOND

F elix was looking at her. Really searching her face. Aria could almost see the cogs turning in his mind, the cogs that would produce the answer to her question she hadn't really asked him. Eventually his lips began to move and aria instructed her ears to listen.

"Aria, when I went through the portal everything changed. I almost spent three months thinking I wasn't going to see any of you again and after loosing luke once, I had to switch myself off from the feeling of losing him again." He paused, " and then I went to the future where, lets just say, Luke isn't around"

Aria's stomach lurched. She felt sick, what did that mean? Had he died? Had he runaway? Left? She refrained from asking felix though because she knew that he wouldn't tell her.

" its strange for me to autally got used to the fact that luke isn't gone. And I "

He broke off. Looking away from her. He was holding the now crumbled note that aria had written for him in his hands. Aria wanted to talk to him about it but she couldn't think of the words.

" I get it felix. I haven't known luke for as long as you have but I was there when he died, I was there when he came back and I was there when-"

She stopped. Remembering the rooftop and the seconds that included felix running towards billie, his hands ready to pull her hands off of alice's strugaling body. In the weeks that followed, luke wouldn't shut up about how odd it was that felix would actively stop him from saving alice and put himself in lukes place. Aria had said to him then that felix was just trying to protect him but now that she was actually alone with felix, actually able to ask, her mind itched for her to say the words.

" felix, before you went into the portal, billie was dragging alice to the enterance and luke went to save her but you pushed him back and saved her yourself"

His eyes flickered up to hers again, and she could see that he was surprised to be asked such a simple question. But it wasn't a simple question to her or to luke or even to alice who had swore blind that felix would've never saved her from being taken if it hadn't benifited him in someway.

" so why did you save her ? alice I mean" she asked softly, not wanting the accent of pure nosiness ruin her causal tone. Felix laughed almost shyly like he hadn't even thought that saving her had been a problem.

" why wouldn't I ?" he asked. Matching aria's caual tone.

Aria just raised her eyebrows at him. "Because you *hate* her"

Felix lowered his head almost shamefully " I knew that if I didn't save her, luke would and I couldn't loose him again."

Aria nodded her head almost without meaning too, it did make sense realisticly because even though felix and alice had there differences would they really be willing to let the other person die or be taken away from someone they loved?

Aria didn't know how to feel, somehow she'd come in here ready to pick apart all that she saw wrong with felix, all of the parts that had changed but now as she stared at his bend head, at the blackness of his hair, the freckle in the crock of his neck she realized that she didn't need to. For whatever reason her future self had changed him and whatever she'd done or said doe that to happen was going to happen eventually. She'll know what the future holds one day she just couldn't stand not knowing now, when she could have a chance at changing it.

Aria thought then, her eyes drifting to the swirling red and gold sunset out the window, even if she wanted to she could get the truth out of felix, get the except days, weeks months account of everything that had happened but she couldn't help but see the sadness wolling in his eyes everytime she caught a glimpse of them, couldn't help but feel the pity, the utter diress that came off him in waves when he was sat siclently like this. If He didn't want to talk of the events that were coming and the girl in the future who was, at the end of the day, her ,didn't want her knowing then what right did she have to force it.

Aria knew that the people she loved would die, surely that was enough for her to not want to know anything more? Her mind burned, her blood boiling at the thought. All she could do now was protect the people in her life and make sure the future and whatever it had in store for them, didn't come true.

Something in her pocket buzzed and she reached into it expecting it to be her phone. Instead she pulled out the match box device that Billie had given her, she had thought she'd given it back. There was a dot on the screen when she opened it up and she couldn't help but gasp when she saw it. Felix looked up at her confused for a second before he saw what she was looking at.

" is that –" he asked shuffling closer to her.

" the location of the 2nd evolver" she said, almost in a whisper. They were looking at each other gleefully and she had to remind herself that felix already knew who that dot represented. He was smiling slightly like he knew what she was thinking and as she looked down at the map that had appeared on the screen aria was sure she saw him lean forwards so that now he was only a few itches away from her forehead. She could feel his breath on the top of her head, it stirred her hair and aria couldn't help but sense that if she were to look up, there faces would be millimetres apart from touching.

"where does it say they are?" Felix asked, the breath that came with his words caused her Goosebumps of excitement to fade slightly.

She looked, trying to work out the maps location on the map of the world she'd got in her head. After a few seconds it finally clicked and another flurry of butterflies emptied into her stomach.

"America" she said finally after rechecking her answer over and over in her head. "They're in America"

* * *

The academy's canteen was massive and Brendon hadn't stepped foot in it since most of the academy members had been killed by the criminals populating the hill view prison. There hadn't been a need for it, the thirty remaining members ate either in their rooms or on the go while on patrol.

But things were changing now. He flicked on the lights and they fluttered a few times before washing the whole room with an artificial light that you would only get in a classroom or a hospital. It shone down on the tables and the stools that surrounded them, dead flowers were placed in the centre of some of them, the giant glass windows that you couldn't see from the outside, had black, velvet curtains cast over them.

His boots made sounds on the white tiled floor and the thudding sound they made echoed around the walls and bounced off the double doors that led to the kitchen.

It was weird too see all the stools that had once been filled with people all talking and eating together. It was weird to see them empty and now with just over three months of the room being boycotted, it was even weirder to think that this room with this many seats used to be full.

The kitchen was cold and Brendon felt sick at the thought that maybe some of the food that had been served on the last day before everyone had left for the prison, which was macaroni cheese if he remembered correctly, had been left in the serving containers. The air smelt old like it had been untouched for decades not just for a few months and Brendon felt the same shiver of unease as if he was back in a place that hadn't been used in years. He went into the walk in fridge that was situated right at the back of the kictchen, it was colder in here of course and he hadn't brought with him a jacket. He rubbed his bare arms as he scanned the shelves looking for something that remotely resembled a 'declan came home and we found out that he's one of the evolvers that will help kill the end of the world and we found more magic people and they will also help us also luke isn't dead' celebratory meal. He eyed the frozen leg of lamb on the bottom shelf and couldn't help thinking that lamb just wasn't going to cut it, especially now that they had their Texan guests to cater for.

He sighed. Things had gotton crazier in the last few days and even he had thought that they'd just got into the swing of things, aria and alice were just understanding the basics of running the place and the patrols had gotton to the stage where everyone just excepted them for what they were, but now things had gotton stepped up a notch, that notch very recently being blown to pecies by the locaton of the 2nd evolver being discovered.

Aria had wanted to leave for america immediately and as much as Declan was eager to find out who was going to join them in there epic quest, he had suggested that they wait a day or two for people to rest . he had also stated very heavily that nothing else was going to happen until he had his welcome home party, which everyone, including aria was more than up for. So here he was, in the cold freezer of the acadmeys canteen trying to decide weither a frozen chicken or frozen steak was going to be best for a party where not only were the magically enlightened invited but an evil immortal who was only going to be there because she had, pleasurably gatecrashed.

" I would suggest both the streak and the chicken" alice said apperaring out from behind the cupboard that held the cheese, milk and butter. Brendon jumped and collided with the pans hanging off the wall behind him. He swore at her but she couldn't hear over her own laughter.

Brendon righted himself and scowled at her " yes, hilarious" he said, shoving her aiside.

" its not my fault your scared of me" she said, a smile on her face and laughter still painted in her eyes.

He turned to look at her his eyebrows raised. " alice, everyone is scared of you, did you not see the poor Texan boy you practically scared into keeping quiet" he couldn't help but chuckle at the image of the teenage boy flinch under the very gaze of Alice's anger. Not many people liked alice but everyone respected her, that's what had made her a good leader along side aria who was born to lead weither she liked it or not.

" legend has it, that boy who fell silent under the very gaze of alice taylor" he leaned in close so that he was centimetres from alice'ss face " never spoke again" he said in a dramatic whisper.

Alice just batted him away although she was smiling. " you watch way to many horror films" she said fondly.

Brendon had turned back to the shelves of meats and was in the process of picking up a big slab of steak

" and you train too hard"

"training hard isn't a bad thing, we all need to train hard to be good, better" she said, following him as he walked back out into the kitchen, the slab of meat in his hands.

" and we all need to watch horror movies to be prepared for the horrors of life" he said, placing the meat on one of the kitchen sides and walking over to the 'veg counter'

" the horrors of life?" she questioned, mockery in her voice. Alice had gone over to the knife's rack and picked up two suitable knifes to chop the carrots and broccoli brendon had acquired from the piles of veg they had available to them.

" the name of my upcoming spin off series" brendon announced, his voice imitating a movie trailer esk commentator

" spin of series of what?" alice asked, joinging him at the kitchen counter by the door, chopping boards were all ready in front of them.

" my life, this series is about the horrors of it" brendon announced again, bringing the knife down on the carrots head. Killing it instanty. Alice was doing the same with the stem of broccoli she was holding down in one hand.

" riiiight, anyway watching horror movies isn't bad its just not going to better you at fighting" alice said in her sarcastic tone that suggested that she didn't actually care for the subject anymore she was just saying what she was to annoy him.

" okay so what are you going to do if a werewolf comes flying at you?" he asked her, a genuine question he liked to ask when and if he was ever let out to speak to the human public.

"nothing because werewolves don't exist" Alice said, disappointment plain in her tone. Alice as much as everyone at the academy was regularly disappointed by the lack of evidence that such creatures existed, they had heated conversations about it at least once a week and not a single one of the people who attended the academy could come up with a reason as to why werewolf weren't real. If vampires could exist then why couldn't humans that could turn into wolfs. That was Brendon's argument anyway.

" oooh you said that with your chest, there is no proof than they don't" he argued then, knowing that alice as much as anyone, would happily ditch everything to go and find some evidence, even if she had to make it herself.

" fine, if a werewolf was coming at me I would stab it with a silver dagger, you don't need to watch horror movies to know that" alice said triumphantly as she scraped the chopped up broccoli she had on her board into the pan at the stove next to her. He hadn't even realised she'd even turned it on and by the look of the hissing pieces of vegtable in it, put water in it to boil.

" what if a vampire comes at you then? And you cant say they don't exisit" he said, chopping his carrot in time with his words to emphasise them. He waited for her response because he also knew alice had a soft spot for those creatures.

" the problem with that one is the horror movies tell it wrong, wooden daggers aren't the only weapon that can kill them and they don't suck the blood out of people oh and the BIG mistake is that they aren't even people"

" ah your forgetting –" he cut in, shaking his head playfully.

" well obviously carilgo doenst count as a vampire" she

said, her voice suddenly defensive " hes the maker of them yes but he isn't scary what so ever" she had committed to stirring the pot and once again brendon hadn't noticed but she had taken all the chopped up bits of carrot he'd been cutting and had put them in the pot she was now adjusting the heat for.

" so your telling me if your in a fight with carligo you wouldn't be scared or even remotely worried?" brendon was sure that if anyone was in a fight with anyone you would have to be at least a little bit scared, especially when in one with a vampire.

Alice thought about this for a second and brendon could see he had her stubbed " well of course he's part of the end of the world, I actually can't win against him no matter how hard I trained because im not an evolver"

Of course she had found a loop hole to his question, nothing could deny the fact that she would lose whatever she did to caligo.

" I feel you, I guess sometimes being 'not an evolver' is a good thing" he said, defeat in his voice he hadn't realised he'd put there. " you do realise we've just had a conversation about caligo using facts we don't even know are true when we have someone upstairs who actually knows him" brendon continued walking over to the island in the middle of the kitchen and resting his elbows on its surface, in the centre of this island was a stack of recipe books that he'd never actually opened. Alice came over, dragging a old wooden stool with her. She sat on it leaning over so her elbows were resting on the island's surface.

" are you suggesting we go ask billie about one of her

mates so we can settle a debate whether horror movies are useful as training or not?" alice asked him her eyebrows rasied.

" well I was just saying it as a wow moment"

" a *wow* moment?" alice said covering her hands with her face, when she took them away again her cheeks were wet from her tears of laughter " you've been spending too much time with aria's mum"

She squealed as Brendon leaned over and lovingly kicked her in the shin.

CHAPTER 17
GONE

Caligo had a hangover. Not an alcohol-related one either, although he had to his surprise managed to neck 5 pints of beer at the pub last night with spiral James before resorting to feeding on its residence. His head was pounding, and he didn't feel up to listening to spiral James's stories and/or possible information that might change everything or at least that's what the text had said anyway. The room he was sat in was filled with science machines, and generic test tubes sat on the dust-covered tables. He hated it in this room. It reminded him of boredom.

The lights in the room were blinking on and off, and the buzzing of the flies and wasps that were stuck in the out casing that covered the lights were beginning to really piss Carligo off. After what felt like 300 years, spirals wobbly figure, walked through, or to put it more accurately fell through the door to his lab. The smile on his face was doing little to persuade caligo that good news was on the agenda.

"you look awful" they both said to each other at the same

time. caligo raised his eyebrows, questioning that fact even when spiral had finally sat down.

" what's going on? Why have you made me wait in your increasingly smelly and boring lab ?"

spiral just grinned "oh its good"

"why isn't malus here? if this news is so good, surely you should tell him."

"I will, but you know what he's like, he will want to do something straight away."

"and we don't because?.." caligo questioned, getting irritable.

" because Felix is back from the future"

"right? what does that mean for us?"

"It means that he knows a lot more than we know, it means that we need to get him back" spiral James was drumming his fingers on the table excitedly.

" thats easy right, I can send my vampires to the academy and -"

"that will work as a distraction but planting some vampires around there base isn't going to stop them, you know that. They need evolvers. luckily for us, we have the one thing they need to find them."

"the matchbox" caligo confirmed nodding his head." so we can just find the evolvers before them, get rid of them and steal Felix back while Aria creed and her friends are weakened"

"precisely" spiral james was up, rooting around the cupboards in his lab. He seemed inpatient now like things were 'not where they were supposed to be.

" and where is it?" caligo asked, not caring enough to get up from his seat and help his friend look." I dont know, I left it right here"

"well, who else knew it was there?"

"I was in here with Billie a few weeks ago, ma-" spiral paused the colour from his face draining. he swore. "what?" caligo was annoyed now.

" I overhead aria and Felix talking, Billie is with them at the academy, I dont know if she's there because shes undercover or because -"

"because she's working against us?" caligo wasn't surprised Billie was always the one to go against the rules, "so you think she took it?" spiral slammed his hand down on one of the lab's surfaces.

" yes, and she's going to wish that she hadn't"

CHAPTER 18
GONE WRONG

The sword was pointed at aria's throat. it dug sharply into her skin and aria could feel her blood trickle slowly down her neck. She closed her eyes, breathing in the thick musty air around her. She concentrated on it, allowing for the cool flow of the winds outside to make their way through the vents attached onto the wall beside her and wrap themselve's around her fingers. Aria breathed out, allowing for the thin wraps of air to intertwine their way up her arms, the pumping blood in her veins cooling at its touch. The air around her hands felt so solid now that it was like she could-

She grabbed it. Her eyes snapped open, the light from the low lights up above glinted off the swords edges and the handle seemed to glow as alice stared at her from behind it. Her arm was outstretched, the sword tightly gripped in it. She could see the sweat on Alice's biceps and knew that the weight of the sword must be burning her muscles but still her arm didn't waver or even shake.

Her skin was starting to buzz lightly and it started too, like it always did, spread to the whole of her body. She felt like a charged battery and the strands of air she was now holding in her hands seemed to vibrate with her, willing to be used.

Aria looked once at Declan who was leaning against the far wall of the training room, his eyes keen on seeing how the next few seconds were going to play out. Aria knew he was looking to see some improvement in her fighting and now she knew that he was one of her team of evolvers, she wanted to impress him even more.

Aria stepped back so the knife was no longer at her throat, almost instantly the world around her seem to slow down so her movements were the only thing moving normally. She flug her hands up above her head intending for her whips of air to lash out at Alice like the reigns of a horse. They struck her and sent her stumbling backwards. Aria run forwards, ducking a slashing blow from Alice's sword and another flying kick that sent aria rolling. She landed in a crouch a metre or so away from Alice and kicked out, turning her body at the same time so that she looked like a cog moving in a clock. Everything may have been in slow motion but Alice was fast and jumped landing behind aria. She turned and threw a punch that connected with Alice's jaw sending her head rocking back. Aria stepped in and flipped Alice over her hip so that she landed face down on the floor. She stood over her, breathing heavily her heart thumping melodically in her chest.

She blinked. Alice was there before she had even got her eyes opened fully. She head-butted her and Aria stepped back bringing her hands up to block the kick Alice swung her way. Aria japped and hit alice's shoulder and then she was gone.

Aria gasped as a knee was slammed into her back sending all the breath out of her lungs. Alice spun her so that they were now facing each other. Alice was smiling and fainted high making aria raise her hand up to block a slash of her sword she thought she was going to hit her with, instead she went low and kicked at aria's knee sending her to the floor, before she could reach it however Alice grabbed her waist and threw her to the far wall.

Aria hit the brick with a hard thud and slipped down it, coughing. She closed her eyes resting her head against the cool surface behind her waiting for the dizziness to fade.

" aria you haven't improved since the last time I saw you train" Declan was saying his voice echoing around the open space of the training room. "and that was two months ago"

" well im sorry ive been abit too busy running the place" she said, her head was pounding and a nauseous feeling had crept into her stomach. " anyway alice hadn't been training either"

" and yet she was still better than you" aria could just imagine the idiotic smirk Declan had on his face now but she didn't have the energy to open her eyes to see it.

" she's been training for ten years" aria shouted faintly at him, opening her eyes to glare at him. He had started to walk towards alice and her now, his arms crossed over his red corduroy dungarees.

" you didn't use any of the techniques I showed you and what was that trick with the wind? There was barely any power behind it" his voice sounded exasperated like this was the worst thing that could've possibly happened in the last two months he was gone.

" aria, you were fine. You've been doing this for three

months and you've already leant more than expected"
Alice's voice was light and concern was glinted in her
eyes. Alice was rarely nice to anyone but aria knew she
did have a soft spot for her even if she had thrown her at a
wall. Aria got shakily to her feet, feeling to make sure her
unused sword was still in her belt where she had left it. It
was and it seemed to weigh her down as she approached
the others, as if to remind her of her defeat.

" I haven't been training with my magic because im
scared im going to loose control like I did at the prison"
her voice got lower as it reached the end of the sentence
and the nausea that had appeared in her stomach a moment ago resurfaced as she thought of Eddie's cracked
broken body.

" that's okay, I know Declan hasn't been around to teach
you and look over your session but he won't leave again"
she was looking at Declan as if she was telling him as well
as aria " you'll be back to the formidable aria we all know
and love in no time"

" why can't you be this nice to me" Declan said pouting
with sad eyes, alice just rolled her own at him.

" I wasn't that bad though was i?" aria asked, rubbing her
throat where the sword had been held. She had directed
the question at alice because she already knew how Declan felt about her performance. He answered anyway.

" yes"

"no" alice said, glaring at Declan and his response.

" maybe it will help you if you see me fight someone else,
like a fight show and tell although I need someone different to fight, brendon wont be good because ive faught
him too many times and that wont teach you anything

about switching it up"

" switching it up?" aria questioned, crossing her arms.

" yeah, that's your problem I think, you stick to much to the training drills you've been taught. To a person that hasn't faught before that's great but to someone who has…" she let her voice trail off.

" you'll be the most predictable person to fight on the planet" Declan finished.

" so I need to train how to look like I haven't trained" she looked at them both, baffled " sounds easy"

" did someone say they needed someone to fight?" a soft Irish voice projected itself from the door way. They all knew who it was of course.

Felix was walking towards them, he was wearing a long sleeve black t-shirt that hugged his arm muscles, his jeans matched and as black as his outfit was it would never and could never match the absolute and complete stalk blackness of his hair which was flopped limply in front of his face liked a shield. The felix she had known three months ago would've never let his hair look as scruffy as this and aria couldn't help but add this to the mental list she had of reasons why the future had changed him.

Alice had a mischievous glint in her eyes as he approached.

" Félix you want to fight Alice?" Declan asked not hiding his surprise.

" well she's not going to fight *you*" Felix retorted coming to a stop next to her.

" she would lose" Declan said giving alice a knowing look,

she punched his arm but didn't deny it as felix went to grab a sword from the wall in which they were displayed. Alice walked so she was facing him and they were only a few metres apart.

Aria walked so that she was stood a safe distance away beside Declan. Who was, she could tell, very excited. It amazed aria that these two hadn't faught before considering there feud

" go" Declan said loudly and the sound of clinking swords started, she watched as they flipped and kicked and slashed at each other and she couldn't help the whirl of nerves that she felt watching. She looked at Declan.

" declan" she said looking at him, he looked back at her a question in his eyes. " America, when are we going? We can leave in the next few hours?" she asked, hopeful.

He smiled at her, " aria I think its best if we wait till morning, we're all tired and it wont hurt to wait, plus ive heard brendon is cooking us up a nice 'celebratory' meal tonight and personally i don't want anyone to miss it"

He must've seen the disapointment in her eyes as he added quickly " I know you want to get all the evolvers together fast but if you rush it something will go wrong, whoever this evolver is will still be there tomorrow."

Aria just nodded, her voice to dry to say anything. So Declan continued " and also when I say 'we' I mean you, alice, felix and billie. Brendon will stay with me here"

She felt her heart contract in panic " what? You're not coming with us ? and you want me to take billie?"

" the end of the world will expect her to be here with felix so sending her away with you guys to America means they wont have a reason to come here. By the time they do realise your there, you'll be back here, besides I need to be here to make sure all the people from the texas clan get here and settled in okay, you'll be fine aria." he said it so nonchalantly that aria just couldn't believe the words he was saying. Anything could happen while they were away and as silly as it seemed, she saw Declan as the adult, as the person who could fix everything and know what to do.

" tomorrow." She said hoarsely a nervous lump had formed in her throat but she nodded at him none the less. It did make sense, he needed to be here.

A few moments pasted before Declan spoke again." aria? Have you seen your mother recently?"

Aria couldn't help but flinch, that question just proved that the wall she had built around that part of her life wasn't as stable as she thought. She blushed not too sure if she was embarrassed at the question or by the answer which was a big fat 'no'.

She didn't know why but she just couldn't bring herself to go and visit her mum and all her old friends. Of course she had spoken to them on the phone and had informed them all that she was staying at the black box academy but something about seeing them face to face made her stomach tie itself in knots.

" well I think you should go visit her, just to tell her that you'll be going away for a few days. Just so that she doesn't come here to see you. Bring brendon with you" he added and aria just looked at him.

" I was planning on it " she said, fully aware that her mum had grown to like brendon out of everyone because he was the only one who actually spoke to her when she came to visit her at black box, despite the fact that the place was meant to be a secret and despite the fact that everytime she visited aria was either on patrol or in a meeting, her mother came to visit her at least once a week. Or at least now she came to visit brendon because aria couldn't bing herself to face her own mother out of quilt. The more she spent time around these people the more she could feel herself beginning to undertsnad why her father left them. This world, these people, it was easy to loose yourself in it and she just couldn't shake the feeling that she was slowly starting to detach herself from her old life. Like her father had done.

She turned her attention back to the fight going on infront of them. As aria watched she saw a multitude of cuts litter felix's body and as she looked she could see that they weren't disappearing. She could sense Declan tense next to her and even alice seemed to stop what she was doing and look at him in dismay.

Declan was already half way to felix by the time aria pieced together what this meant. " felix, you're not healing?" she voiced her realization.

" yeah I told you I don't heal anymore" felix said, a look of surprise on his face like he couldn't think why this was a big deal.

" you still have magic in your blood right?" Declan asked, looking at felix like he had never seen him before.

" of course," felix said, defensively

" then.." alice started, gesturing to the whole of his cut bleeding body with the tip of her sword " what's all this"

His eyes flickered to them all before resting his gaze on

her. He sighed " you know of the insane right, well there blood, if it gets into you somehow then-" he gulped and aria noticed that he had started sweating "it infects you"

" how does it infect you?" aria asked and felix looked at her with a knowing look in his eyes like he'd asked the same question before.

" well, it does something to the magic in our blood and somehow stops you from healing fast like your meant too." He paused looking off into the distance " along with many other things" his voice was distant.

" so how did you get infected?" alice asked, her eyes scanning his body like she was annoyed that him of all people could be hurt.

" this" felix bend down and rolled up his trouser leg, revealing the long jagged cut going down the lengh of his right leg. They'd all seen it before but still the sight of it made aria's stomach flip.

" that was done by one of the insane?" Declan asked shaking his head, " god, well at least we know what to expect from them now" he had gone quite pale and aria knew they were all shocked at the propect of facing these creatures sometime In the future.

Before felix could reply the doors to the training room slammed open, causing for the handles to slam into the walls behind them. Brendon was running towards them, sweat was pouring down his face and as he stopped he placed his hands on his knees trying to get some breath in his lungs to actually talk.

They all watched as billie walked casually in behind him, she regarded brendon with a disgusted look before walking round him, her hands clasped together like a news reporter. She smiled at them all. It sent chills down her spine.

" hello, fellow good people I am here to inform you that my end of the deal has been carried out"

" you mean-" aria began

" the criminals are gone?" alice finished and aria couldn't help but notice that they needed to stop finishing each other sentences like they were twins.

Billie just nodded and aria couldn't help the feeling of relief that sweaped her, she faught the urge to go over and high five her. She doubted billie would appreciate that much and aria still wanted all ten of her fingers.

" so what's up with him" felix said pointing at the still panting brendon behind her.

Billie looked back at the panting figure " oh yeah and there may be some bad news he wants to share with you"

They all looked at him as he stood up to face them all. The three words he said next sent aria's bubbling panic that was already brewing in her stomach burn almost as bright as brendons cheeks.

"Vampires" he said, through ragged, uneven breaths "they're everywhere"

CHAPTER 19
GONE ROUGE

"**W**hat are you doing here?" Luke said, jumping at the sight of Ryan standing in dim lights of the hallway. "who are you? Like really?" Ryan asked, his face unamused. He started to amble towards luke, and he was glad to see he had no weapons on him that he could see.

"im luke Quinn, what are you talking about?" he said, trying to keep his tone casual and confused which was hard to do when he knew that Ryan knew something was wrong.

"im talking about the fact that your planning to kidnap me" Ryan was only four metres away now. Luke could see the strange and abstract glint of something close to fear in his eyes. The kid was brave, he gave him that. "what? Im not-"luke started, trying not to blush at the accusation that was all too true, what how did he know?

"I heard your conversation with aria on the phone" Ryan said as if he'd heard luke's thoughts. Luke just looked at him, Ryan practically recoiled at aria's name and the fact that he heard that conversation must have meant Ryan had been following him. Luke made his face look bemused and put his hand up to his face, pinching the bridge of his nose.

"are you stupid?" luke asked him, shaking his head.

"sorry, im not-"

"you overheard someone talking about how they were going to kidnap you" luke walked over to Ryan, pointing at him like he'd put his hand up in class wanting to answer a question. "and you, instead of running away you actually went to your alleged kidnapper's house and confronted them?"

Ryan was just looking at him astonished. "god it's like you want to be kidnapped" luke said, clamping his hand onto Ryan's shoulder making him jump. Ryan shook his head as if shaking loose luke's words.

"yeah well, I just wanted to know why" Luke sighed, clearly this was now the time to tell Ryan the truth, it was better than actually having to kidnap him because as the records show, he wasn't very good at it and without Felix to help or anyone, luke was sure it was going to end badly anyway. So he turned, walking into the kitchen gesturing for Ryan to follow him. "okay fine let me just explain"

The kitchen was small but placed on one wall was a bar area with three old bar stools placed next to it, luke sat and watch as Ryan did the same.

"explan?" Ryan questioned, his eyebrows knitted together.

"yeah, explain that im, not an evil criminal come to keep

you, hostage, I just need your help" luke couldn't help the slight hint of desperation that was evident in his voice, he hadn't realised it, but the idea of finally actually telling the truth made him understand how much he needed Ryan to come back with him.

"so why didn't you just ask me?" Ryan asked, his face slightly annoyed looking like the prospect of luke actually being an evil criminal hadn't actually crossed his mind until now.

"well, to be honest, if I ask you to help, there is a chance you will say... no" luke had started tapping on the top of the bar with his fingers, only looking at Ryan when he said his next bit

"and I can't really take no for an answer" He saw Ryan shift slightly on his chair in the corner of his eye and luke couldn't help thinking that he wouldn't blame Ryan If he made a run for it.

"that is exactly what an evil criminal would say" Ryan just muttered. Luke looked up at him then, trying to see in his eyes, the answer to this whole situation in them. There was no way of knowing except for just asking so luke cleared his throat,

"do you know?"

"uh, do I know what?" Ryan asked, confusion clouding his eyes. Luke shook his head

"don't make me say it"

"well I think im going to have too" Ryan said, failing to hide the smirk brewing on the corner of his mouth. Luke couldn't help but notice the lack of confrontation in the conversation.

"fine but please don't think im a nutter" he said running his sweaty hands through his hair.

"a nutter?" Ryan was actually trying not to laugh now, the corners of his eyes were creased,

"yeah like im insane, anyway what im asking is are you magic?" luke squinted his eyes at Ryan as if trying to see the potential fragments of his blood that could contain it.

"what?" Ryan was suddenly very still, and his face was frozen in a soft state of annoyed puzzlement "is this some sort of a British joke?"

"come on, don't play dumb, there is no way you can play basketball like that and not you know have the elements' help'" luke said throwing his hands up in frustration, he knew that there was magic in this boys veins. He just couldn't help but feel the Deja vu of the situation. Aria had had the same look on her face when they'd told her although luke hadn't found that quite as frustrating.

"the elements?" Ryan said, smirking ever so slightly at him.

"oh lord, you really don't know?" he said, trying not to sound too disappointed. The prospect of having to explain everything about who he was and what Ryan should expect bore weight he didn't want to put on this boy who was so close to having a normal life. After all, they'd told aria, and a day later she was caught in an explosion that simultaneously sparked her magic off. The fact was he wasn't 100% sure that Ryan was magic. Still, he wasn't 100% that he wasn't so luke got up gripping the bottle of sambuca that Declan had left out and took a big swig of it skewing his face up at the aftertaste. When he had swallowed he held out the bottle to Ryan for him to take.

"if you want to know everything, you'll need a shot of this" he waited for Ryan to take it, when he didn't luke shook it at him raising his eyebrows "trust me"

Ryan just shook his head in disbelief "it can't be that bad and if it is why do you think I would be able to help?" There was a sort of humming energy between them that luke knew if he allowed it to consume him, he would be able to manipulate it. Ryan didn't seem to notice it though which did help luke come to the conclusion that he didn't know anything about luke's world. Luke turned so Ryan wouldn't see his face and the look of guilt that was etched on it. The only way he was going to be able to make Ryan understand was to bring him back to the academy, and the only way Luke was capable of doing that was by making him. He turned, his hand out as he walked quickly across the room. Ryan wasn't even aware of luke's hands around Ryan's throat until the sleepers hold took effect and Ryan slumped off the stool and lifeless into luke's arms.

* * *

The van that Declan had purchased smelt of brunt tires and rust, luke found this mildly amusing as he placed Ryan in the back of it. Luckily the nighttime brought a nice coolness to the air that felt gentle against his skin. It felt like almost too calm and quiet to be dragging a body into a back of a van and luke couldn't help but wonder what aria would say if she was here, probably something about how he was kidnapping Ryan wrong. His mind instantly then went to Felix, and a pang of sadness spread in his stomach. He didn't like to think of his brother because he missed him too much, the fact that he was probably suffering a fate worse than death made his blood run cold after all what could a group of immortals possibly be doing with Felix? He closed the van doors, making sure all of Ryans limbs were all safely inside. There was a stone already digging into luke's foot, and he had to resist the urge rip his boot off right then and there. He needs to get out of here before rya woke up and could make a run for it. The engine came to life as Luke turned the keys in the ignition, and the food crumbs on the dashboard vibrated slightly.

❆ ❆ ❆

Ryan had woken up half an hour ago. That wasn't without the stereotypical 'trying to get Luke to stop driving the van routine' which had resulted in Luke slapping Ryan so hard he'd given up and retreated to the passenger's seat, all signs of a protest gone. This was lucky because Luke couldn't stand to be made to serve into the opposite lane anymore, the police did not need to be called for Ryan's silly 'I don't want to be kidnapped' charade. Which was starting to get old now.

CHAPTER 20
THE SCHOOL RUN

This wasn't a good idea. The storm that had been brewing for the past few days whipped and lashed out around Brendon's head. Despite the new threat of vampires, he wasn't carrying any weapons with him. The oversized black puffer coat he was hugging around him wasn't going to do much against the sharp fangs and spikes of any aria and him encountered on their way to the school. Aria was some ways behind him, and even though the wind was roaring in his ears he could still hear the consistent complaints coming from the evolver, she was wearing a long black trench coat that didn't look warm or remotely practical.

Brendon couldn't help but imagine what they looked like, two of the world's most perfect protectors who would probably die of cold or mild hyperthermia before they could even get a chance to face up to any of caligo Bellator's creatures. The buildings and cars were shrouded in a dense fog that made it hard to see much in the way ahead of them, this Brendon couldn't help pointing out to Aria every time she suggested they go back, was something they needed to be out in to really understand its purpose. It wasn't a usual fog it had a smell to it that could only be described as the smell of the dead. Or the living dead as Aria had kindly pointed out. The streets were a mess, and if Brendon hadn't known better he would be sure that a bomb had been dropped on this part of the country, buildings were mostly ruined with walls missing, and cars were flipped, and some were scorched like they been set on fire. He was about to stop so Aria could catch up when he heard her gasp and shout his name, seemingly at the same time. He turned to look at her, the wind blowing the hair out of his face and stinging his cheeks. Even with the fog and the bright red of her cheeks washing out the pigments in her skin, she looked pale, her hand clasped tightly over her mouth. She was looking off to the side, where the sides of the bridge they were walking across would be if the mist wasn't obscuring Brendon's vision. He didn't know what he expected to see when he looked to see what Aria was groping at, but The ripped open bodies of the local police department weren't on the list. They were strung up on the railing like plastic dolls, and the words' evolving doesn't mean you'll survive" were written across them in a black substance. He had to force the bile that rose in his throat down, and it burned as he found his way to Aria's side. She looked up at him not hiding the tears that were trying not to spill over her eye sockets.

"do you think that-" she began her lip quivering. "no, I don't think the criminals would've of written that. The bodies look to fresh to be anything they did, in fact.." he trailed off as he neared them, the sleeve of his coat covering his nose. He didn't get to finished his sentence because he found himself suddenly rotating backwards in the air. It took him a second to realise he was flying through the air and that id he didn't right himself he would probably land on his neck. He twisted in the air and almost as soon as he'd found himself In the air, he was back on the ground, only just landing in a crouch his hand springing out to right himself against an overturned car. He heard, aria scream and then he was running through the fog, squinting his eyes to see what was going on.

"aria?" he called out, the mist had definitely gotten thicker, and almost everything over a metre away from him was covered.

"Brendon? Where's the vampire?" she called back, from his right. Vampire? Was that what had flung him? "uh I don't know, but we shouldn't be split up" he said trying not to let the momentary lack of sight panic him. "one sec" Aria said and then a wave of air blew at him, knocking and clearing the space in front of him from the fog. Aria walked to his side, rubbing her hands together like she was trying to get crumbs of them. A shriek sounded from behind them, and they both whirled. The lack of weapons they carried was made even more apparent when they both instinctively reached into their empty weapons belts under their coats. Aria swore, and Brendon couldn't help but gasp at the massive creature in front of them. His Skelton like spider legs were massive one was easily as long as he was, the snarling humanlike face it carried was decorated in spikes. The eyes were plain and milky like a piece of paper being washed away by the rain. The torso of the creature was slashed and pale, its shoulders covered in bite marks and iridescent residue that Brendon couldn't help but think was blood. It looked disgusting. The creature's fangs were out, of course, and they were long and sharply pointed at the ends. It moved towards them like a scurrying spider, and before Brendon could stop her, Aria was running to meet it.

* * *

She had no weapons she knew that. She had no real sense of what she was doing, she knew that, but yet Aria still found herself running towards the vampire-like she did indeed possess all these things. The tingling in her palms had started, and she wasn't sure when or how but she knew she needed to jump, preferably on the creatures back, like Felix had done the first time she'd met one of calligos pets. It wasn't an easy jump, but then again it was a fundamental part of her training, even as she readied herself she felt the air around her connect and suddenly she was whooshing into the air high above the vampires spiky head.

She flipped over, so she handed on its back, it's now thrashing body the only thing she had to cling too. It was slippery, and her boots slid as she wrapped her hands around the creature's neck. Brendon was shouting at her, but the wind made it so that she could only faintly hear his words.

"– fire – "was all she managed to get from him before she was thrown off the back of the creature, she reached out and grabbed one of its legs, she was dangling now her hands grabbed slightly around the smooth, rubbery skin of the spider-like limbs.

She coughed, bile rising in her throat at the pungent smell this monster gave off, it hung in her throat, and she felt like she was suffocating. Bredon was trying to distract the beast with provocative movements, but Aria was sure the creature was blind. Its eyes were unseeing as she reached up and placed her hand on its chest, a warm feeling ignited there, and she closed her eyes and let it grow. The wind cashing around her, the fog damping her hair, she felt it all slow down and pour into her like she was plugged into an IV at the hospital. Her palm was hot, and before she could move her hand away, a blast of flame exploded out and shot into the vampire's chest.

It screeched a deafening sound that echoed around the building they were surrounded by. Aria fell from where she was grabbing on to, and as she readied herself for the impact a sharp slashing sensation scarped across her check, one of the creature's legs and swiped at her. She gasped as she landed hard on the road. Brendon shouted her name, and in her momentary dreamy state from the pain her cut was producing, she saw his figure dart up and plunge his hand in the charred and open hole in the chest of the creature. The vampires gave one finally ear-splitting shriek as its unbeating heart got ripped out and thrown to the floor, the remains of its previous owner's body already erupting into dust around them. She coughed, the dust escaping her lungs.

She felt sick, and the cut left on her cheek still stung. Aria could feel the blood still pouring from it and judging by Brendon's face, it hadn't healed.

"the cut-"brendon began, kneeling down beside her "it hasn't healed yet" She brought her trembling hand to where the vampires spike hard slashed at it, it was wet and warm, and when she brought them away her fingers were covered in blood. Her head surged, and her stomach jumped, Brendon was right, she wasn't healing.

"how? Why? Has this happened before?" she asked Brendon in a gasp. Brendon was staring off somewhere in the distance his eyes glassy, his expression focused. "aria, do you remember what felix was saying, why his cut hadn't healed yet" Aria recalled the conversation in her head, the sight of Felix's gaint gash on his leg made her feel queasy even in memory. She nodded

"yeah, he said that the injuries given by the insane don't heal –" she stopped. Her blood froze. Her mind seemed to empty. Every nerve in her body simultaneously went numb. Aria couldn't move, her breathing had gotten short and rabid, and Brendon was trying to pull her to her feet, to calm her down but in the warm brown of his eyes held the same terror that her body seemed all too persistent infighting.

He knew that she knew that whatever the insane were eight years into the future, the vampires that surrounded them today were only just the beginning of the end of the human race, the academy and eventually the world.

PART TWO.

CHAPTER 21
SAFE BUT NOT REALLY

"Y ou're stupid if you think that was a success" Alice said, stirring her coffee matter of factly. Declan was sat across from her smirking into his sandwich.

"it was, aria got the kick up the bum she needed and" he flung his arm wide, almost knocking his own cup of coffee flying. "we got rid of the criminals"

Alice glared at him almost in shock At his profound inept to advertently miss the point. "yes but perhaps you forgot the part where the vampires have us surrounded" Declan was just smiling at her. An observant glint in his eyes that could only capture the image of pure excitement when he didn't say anything Alice finally snapped.

"god Declan, you've basically sent aria and Brendon to their deaths" she covered her mouth the sudden thought causing her stomach to lurch violently.

"bit dramatic "Declan muttered drily. "and anyway this will be good for them"

"good for them?" Alice was gripping her coffee cup so tightly that any more pressure, she was sure, would be enough for the china to crack.

"Declan if this gets them killed you do realise that you will be forever known as the guy who got the third evolver killed.

"nah if anyone dies because of something I've told them to do, that – "he stood plucking a crisp from the plate in front of them "is no ones fault but there own"

❋ ❋ ❋

The school had always looked sad. Its ivy-covered walls and closed off windows weren't recent accessories to its depressing demeanour. Despite Aria's memories of school being mostly good ones, she couldn't help the shiver that ran up her spine the moment they rounded the corner, bringing the full image of the building she'd been avoiding for months, into view. The thing was she was still technically meant to be attending lessons. The thought of the incoming lecture she was about to ensure just by showing her face here made her deep down wish that the vampire had done more than cut her cheek.

The armed guards were in there usual spots and after a rather relentless battle to stop them from getting medical help for her cut they let her pass. They were nice enough, but Aria could see that they were put out and tired of all this mess. She thought of telling them of the policemen's body's hanging lifeless on the bridge. Still, a burning vile rose in her throat, making her think better of it. That wasn't what they needed right now. Brendon had been quiet next to her the whole journey over here only speaking when there was a loose piece of rubble to traverse or to ask her if her cut had shown any signs of healing yet. It hadn't, and Aria couldn't help notice the panic developing in the pit of her stomach. As far as she was concerned, as soon as they left for America, the sooner they could get together all of the four evolvers and plan a way to save the world. Sadly that involved saying goodbye to her mother... again.

Walking up the path to the front entrance was like the part in a horror film where the main characters approach the haunted house. Aria felt like she shouldn't be here, the space she'd put between herself and this place, between her new and old life were so evident now. Brendon was muttering to himself next to her and Aria glanced at him, his bottom lip was quivering, and she held back the urge to punch him in the arm, he needed to get a grip of himself if they were to make their visit free from any unwanted questions. The door was bolted, and big heavy paddocks dressed it a mesh sort of covering stood in front of it as if the residence inside were captured inside a dog pen. The outskirts of the school were a mess but nothing compared to the carnage of the streets.

"Aria?? What happened to you??" Her mothers desperate and more than worried voice hit her before she could make out her mothers figure in the crowds that populated the gym. There were bunk beds, sleeping bags, even air beds placed in rows with everyone's limited belongings strone around them. Her mother was leaping over the packs of families, her arms frailly franticly until she crushed Aria in a bone defying hug that definitely would leave a bruise.

"what mum? I just fell on the way here" Aria said, finally getting realised from the 'hug'. "did you come alone?" her mum frowned at her, the worry still fixed in her eyes. "brendons getting some food from the canteen" Aria said, trying to look as if she hadn't just fought off a 9 ft vampire on her way to get here.

"oh god Aria, where have you been? I've been worried sick, and it's not like any of those kids at the ... the academy are very helpful" her arms were crossed now, eyebrows raised.

"I know mum, I've been busy, it's not exactly safe to come to visit you and.. things are different now"

"yes, it just has me worried with everything, how did you get here without .. you getting -"

"that's actually what I came here to talk to everyone about" she said, finally turning to see Brendon coming into the gym, she motioned to him to try and get everyone together. after 5 minutes the faces of the town's residence were looking at them, waiting.

"okay so now that everyone is together Brendon and I have some news" Aria began.

Brendon cleared his throat "the criminals are gone but "he said before anyone could cheer too loudly "its still not safe to leave" "why?" a bald man standing near the back shouted, the people around him murmuring like they were thinking the same thing. "there are vampires everywhere" Brendon said dryly. "shut up" Aria hissed elbowing Brendon hard in the rips. The crowd of people in front them were silent and just before Aria could start reassuring them that he was joking a flood of laughter erupted making aria jump. Brendon looked just as astonished as Aria felt, but she couldn't blame them. They were better off thinking that Brendon's warning was a joke than actually believing that vampires existed. They'd started to get up and mill around each other. The flushed face of her mother appeared out of the crowd smiling.

"darling, im so proud, does this mean you're staying?"

she was clearly trying not to sound too hopeful, and that caused the pit in Aria's stomach to open again. "uh, actually mum, im going away for abit" she couldn't look at her mother. She knew she would have tears in her eyes and that, if anything, would be it for Aria. She wouldn't be able to leave if she saw her mother cry. "whwhere? Again really Aria?" her mother's voice was shaking, and Aria had to bite her lip to stop her from looking away from the spot on the floor she'd found. "America" aria whispered, not wanting her mother to hear. "America???" her mother suddenly shouted, causing many of the people trying to leave the hall to turn and look. "Aria what are you playing at? You just said it's not safe to go outside let alone to another country"

"I - "Aria couldn't get the words out. A lump had formed in her throat, and she was scared if she tried to resist it, she would be sick. "I need to mum, you won't understand. It's –"she finally looked up at her mum. Ignoring the pang of guilt, she felt when she saw the look of utter torment on her face.

"its to do with dad" Her mum almost recoiled. They never really spoke of him, and she could see that the fact that she had, meant that her mum was going to let her go. The anger and plain resistance faded from her face,. "who's going with you?" she asked softly. "brendon, alice, Felix and – "she stopped herself, the mention of Billie, someone her mum didn't know and hopefully would never meet wouldn't be very beneficial right now.

"– that's it actually." Her mum just nodded, surprisingly calm at the lineup of people escorting her daughter to another country,

"Aria you have to know that I don't want you to go. But I can't stop you. I just need you to come back safe okay. I don't know what's going on with you at the moment, but you clearly don't want to be here with me, your friends or your family so I won't make you. "she paused, catching her breath. "I hope it's worth it" and with that, her mum, a woman who had watched her and helped her grow up, taught her how to tie her shoelaces. Turned her back on her and started to walk quickly towards the doors.

CHAPTER 22
READY OR NOT

T he water was oddly soft on her skin. It felt like silk, and it glided down her arms and legs, it warmed her face and the cut on her cheek sung slightly, but it wasn't a pain she disliked. The morning sun was prominent as it shone through her bathroom window and landed on the heel of her foot. She liked it, the way it looked reminded her of the two sides of her life, the light part being her private one at the academy, small but the first thing she saw, she thought about. The shadow that surrounded it was bigger, darker and something she avoided. Her old life.

It wasn't that she didn't like who she was or where she used to hang out, the thought of knowing there is a whole other world of excitement to explore would just eat her up, she needed to be here with Alice, Felix, Declan and Brendon, she needed to be a part of something bigger, so she didn't feel so small. Aria closed her eyes again the warm stream of water, her thoughts, regretfully lingering on Luke. Luke Quinn. She shivered, trying to flash past the images of the boy her mind conjured up. Aria missed him so much, and it hurt to see that his brother couldn't share in her sorrow. It was strange regardless of Felix's fears and future life surely that love for his brother should still be there and or more than before. She chewed her lip, this sort of overthinking was what made her want to hide under her covers and never come out. They'd told the others about the cut and how it wasn't healing, Declan was sure that the vampires carligo 'creates' have never been this advanced before. Something was different about them, aria knew that the smell that lingered around the creatures was so off-putting that even the thought of it now made her toes curl.

Felix was quiet when they were disgusting it and that made aria's blood boil the most, the fact that he knew far more about this than anyone else and wasn't giving input was infuriating. She just wished she could shake him and make him tell her everything all the answers they need. But she couldn't. The air was cold when she finally got out the shower, the steam in the mirror was moist as she rubbed it away. Her reflection in the mirror looked tired and worn out, and aria couldn't help but notice she looked like one of those reusable shopping bags that never seem to quite get thrown away. The cut on her cheekbone was sore, and the stitches that had been put in to help the natural healing her body was doing were numb when she prodded at them. Alice was waiting for her on her bed when aria walked out of the bathroom. She looked half asleep, and the suitcases that were laying on the floor at her feet were only half-filled with unfolded clothes.

"you look awful" alice said, her eyes firmly fixed to her phone screen. "you still haven't packed" aria said, rolling her eyes at her. "Declan will confiscate your phone or worse" she waited, going over to sit on the other side of the bed. "he'll stamp on it" Alice just looked up at her, an unamused look on her face. "I would like to see him try and anyway I have packed" she dropped her phone in the open suitcase and bend down to start zipping it up. Aria just shook her head, the thing was they were supposed to be leaving for America in ten minutes. The thought of it terrified her, but the sliver of excitement that raced through her every now and then was electric.

❊ ❊ ❊

The van was loaded up, and Brendon was already in the front seat when aria and alice made it out into the drive-way, suitcase lagging behind them. The morning air was cold but fresh on her skin and her cut stang at the mois-ture in the air. Billie was leaning against the side door of the van, arms crossed her head, leant back on the win-dow.

She wasn't asleep, aria supposed immortals didn't need to sleep, but the slight movement of billies lips gave it away. Aria wasn't close enough to hear what she was say-ing, and something inside her told her that she didn't want too. Felix was pushing his bags into the back of the van, the darkness of the morning blending unnoticed into his hair. When he was done with his bags, he turned and took both Alice's and Arias from there hands. She didn't know why this action surprised her, but she smiled at him all the same. Her coat was wrapped tightly around her concealing the 5 knives she had strapped into her belt, she just hoped that for whatever reason their journey to America wouldn't need a visit from the police. The bulging mass of the matchbox device filled her side pocket, and she couldn't help but notice herself tapping it really, checking it was still there. Brendon was growing impatient in the driver's seat, his voice could be heard rather harshly in the morning haze that surrounded her senses, and she flinched as he screamed at them again to hurry up.

"Jesus, you would think he actually wanted to go on this trip," Declan said from behind them, "Brendon what are you doing? You do realise your not going, don't you?" There was a slamming of a car door and footsteps before Brendon emerged before them out of the gloom "I know, but seriously after the attack on aria you still want just them to go?" he asked casting his hand to indicate the rest of them. Declan had his eyebrows raised the lines of sleep still prominent around his eyes.

"yes. Brendon, I know you don't want to stay here because you know ill make you train. Still, honestly dude" he put his hand on his shoulder "you're impressing no one if you leave," Brendon said nothing but instead stormed off in the direction of the doors. Declan turned to face them, Felix was standing next to her, and she could feel the goosebumps on her right arm stand up.

"okay so you know the plan, get in get the evolver and get out, try to explain little until you get back don't mess around with side plans or missions, this is just a straight journey and back" They all nodded at him, and aria was trying to shake the fact that this felt very much like a lecture her teacher would give before a school trip. She bit back the urge to call him sir as she turned so that it was just Declan and her in the convocation. "Declan, are you sure you'll be okay here like you know they're likely to come here right, the end of the world I mean." Aria couldn't see his face properly in the low light of dust. Still, she could see the moonlight that shined off his eyes in excited sparks. "id like to see em try" was all he said as he patted aria on the back and went to go back inside.

∗ ∗ ∗

Billie was glad that alice wasn't driving, she was also glad that she wasn't being made to chat with anyone on the bus about there plan and the weather. These were both things that had worried her in the build-up to this trip. She was sat at the back, her hands laced together in her lap, her eyes scanning the horizon as they drove along a backcountry road occasionally swerving fallen trees and abandoned cars. Billie didn't know how to feel, but the evil in her expressed a notion of boredom. Yes, they were off to find the second evolver, and yes this was fundamental in her own plan, but somehow Billie just couldn't help but feel underwhelmed.

Something about travelling in a smelly van with three magic folks made her miss the hash comments and smart, elegant cars that she often dealt with back with the end of the world. Felix or Eddie, in her case, was sat on the other side of the van, his hand leaning against the window his eyes shut, and a black beanie pulled over his head. This was somewhat strange to her because the thought of Eddie wearing something so restricting made her want to take a picture and send it straight to the boys to make fun of, but this wasn't Eddie, the boy she'd grown up with, this was Eddie in Felix Quinn's body who, she couldn't help but notice, was starting to act like he maybe just maybe didn't want the world to end.

∗ ∗ ∗

Alice was glad she wasn't driving, the thought of traversing the now treacherous roads to the beach they were heading to make her anxiety fluctuate. Her hands were clammy and her stomach rubbled and growled, reminding her that the cold pasta she'd eaten at 4 am wasn't going to cut it anymore if she wanted to remain focused. She didn't know how the others were feeling but judging from the look on aria's face, they could've all used at least 3 more hours sleep. Alice couldn't stop thinking about the realisation she'd made in the meeting room, of course, she couldn't tell anyone about it just yet because it was merely impossible. All the evidence she had brought up though suggested to her that the second evolver wasn't a far away as they'd all thought and just thinking about the possibility of the person who she thought it was made her almost want to vomit. She looked after at aria once again, looked at the concentration lines that etched her face as she tried to get around yet another crack in the road. Alice couldn't sometimes believe that aria could be deadly, she was so caring and attentive but yet so determined and stubborn to be not left out. Still, alice knew just as much as anyone else how much aria was holding back her lack of control, how much power she really had. Alice just knew that if aria creed couldn't save the world, then they were well and truly screwed.

* * *

Eddie wished he was driving. He needed something to take his mind off the swirling mass of worry that was floating in his head. He wasn't sacred of course Eddie never got scared ever, but something inside him made him want to open the van door and jump out. He was fighting the urge to cry by biting his lip and thinking of a conversation topic that didn't involve recent or current events but somehow talking about what everyone's favourite thing to order from McDonald's was, didn't seem to fit the mood either. So instead he stayed quiet and just hoped that the journey to the pier didn't take long because he didn't fancy being sick in a van next to Billie who would, he knew, make him lick it back off the floor.

* * *

Now aria was fairly sure she shouldn't be the one driving this van. The others seemed to have bagged the back seats by the time she'd gotten in, she didn't mind too much though because she had other things to think about different to the fact that they were about to go to America and find the second evolver and that she had Declan's number on speed dial if they came across anything remotely stressful, e.g. anything to do with social interaction or mild confrontation of any sort. The sun was getting higher. In the sky and with it her hopes seemed to rise, today was the day they found another piece of there puzzle that could potentially stop Felix's future from coming true. She sighed at that thought and looked at the suns morning display for bright orange and red swirls. Maybe just maybe today was the day things started to go right.

CHAPTER
23
HERE I COME

Declan was glad to be at the academy. It was true he missed his home back in Ireland, but something about being around people who were like him made him remember how it felt when he actually attended this school. His heart burned at the memory of Jason creed, his teacher, his mentor someone who he looked up too. His office was still in the same state he'd left it in, and Jason creed was still written on the oak door, no one could bring themselves to take it down even if it wasn't technically his office anymore.

Declan felt weird calling it his own though, and as he sat in the leather swivel chair on the other side of the desk, he felt his body relax finally. The second evolver was in America. He just hoped luke was safe and on his way home, trouble was bound to follow aria and the others over there he just didn't want luke caught up in it, there was enough going here that luke didn't know about. His brother being back was one of them. Declan shook his head, that was going to be an interesting day. It wasn't like Felix was acting like luke Quinn's brother at all, and he knew aria was starting to notice that more than the rest of them. Something was very different about the Quinn boy, and it wasn't just to do with the slight slash of purple that newly decorated his eyes.

"Evolving doesn't mean you'll survive" he muttered the words Brendon had told them that was written on the policemen's bodies. It sounded like a warning but from who? The end of the world weren't that discreet about anything, if they wanted to send a message, they would've done it in a way that left them all petrified. This felt like something different, imminent and Declan cursed himself for not knowing. There was a knock at the door, and Declan took his feet off the desk before shouting "come in" in a tone that he hoped suggested that he was in charge.

Brendon stepped through the doors, shutting them sheepishly behind him. He looked wide-eyed and normally Declan would've noted this to be something of a concern. Still, over the past few days, everyone had that look of complete disability in their eyes. "what's up? "Declan said, placing his doc martens back on the desk, they were blue today with checkered laces. Brendon just shrugged.

"I just think it was a bad idea to send aria away." Declan raised his eyebrows

"and why do you think that? Brendon, she's not safe here, and we both know she would've gone anyway regardless of what anyone told her"

"yes, I know that, but aria needs to understand she cant get what she wants all the time just because she is the third evolver and why is she the third one not the first?" Brendon said his voice growing in confusion. Declan just sighed "the strongest shape is said to be the triangle, the third point is the strongest. So in this triangle of evolvers, I" he pointed to himself "am the first evolver the most grounded, in control, the second point, the second evolver is more skilled and knowledgable. The third is aria, the strongest most powerful, that's why she's important."

"but there are four of you? A triangle doesn't have four sides." "yes but there are four elements. The last evolver is someone who isn't as connected to the rest, but they are needed in order for the elements to work, they are, in a way, the glue that puts us all together."

"sooo they're not really connected to you guys individually, but they're connected to you all as a group?"

"yes so without them we wouldn't have anything to channel our magic through. Each evolver represents one element."

"so do you know what elements you and aria are yet?"

"no, we don't know until we're all together even then it can take a while before we all know for sure"

"damn, that's crazy. So you'll be apart of this all-powerful group while the rest of us just stand around waiting for things to go south" "im afraid there ain't no rest of the wicked in this walk of life"

"no, young Declan. Im afraid there isn't." Declan's eyes flicked to the door at the same time, Brendon spun his head round to do the same. They both froze for a second, unsure of what to do. Malus was stood, in the doorway his figure outlined by the light shining in from the hallway. "interesting, no hello, not even a handshake" Malus shrugged, stepping into the room and closing the door with a short, simple swipe of the hand. Declan found himself rising to his feet.

"Malus? What do you want?" he asked, his voice only

shaking when he said his name. Malus just smiled a weak smile.

"get in, get out, get back. I believe that is your plan for aria and the others was it not?" Declan felt his stomach twist.

"how did you-"he stopped himself, of course, Billie would've told them. She couldn't be trusted after all. "Billie," he said after a short silence.

"ah, yes, Billie. In this case, she hasn't revealed anything of what you guys are up too. In fact, I haven't seen her or Felix in over a week" Malus was looking them both, his red eyes glowing "which leads me to believe you have them captured or worse, you've killed them and-"He held his hand up as if to silence them against there will not talk.

"where have all my beloved criminals gone?" Declan just looked at Brendon who had gone pale under his brown curls.

"uh what do you mean? You don't know what's been going on with the vampires? With Billie?" Malus just stared at him, his face as still as stone.

"if I did, I wouldn't be here asking you, if I did your academy would be nothing but ashes" he cast his hand up, so a book from one of the shelves shot into it. He opened it sharply onto a page Declan couldn't quite get a good look at and smiled. "the criminals are gone. The vampires have you surrounded, and aria creed has found the second evolver" Malus's voice was low, his expression cold. "this could only mean that wherever you've sent them has something to do with this" He turned the book so that the matchbox device that was printed on the page could be seen.

"looks like Jason creed knew more than he let on" They

both leaned forward to stare at the drawing. Declan's heart was hammering in his chest, the image looked exactly like the device Billie had stolen out of carligos lab, but how could that be? Billie had said that caligo had invented that device himself.

"how? That device was invented by carligo Billie said so" Brendon said before Declan could stop him. Malus's eyes lit up all of a sudden, and Declan slammed his hand on the table, almost forgetting where he was.

"Brendon, shut up," he said all too late for it to save the situation.

"ah, I see." Malus said, running his elongated finger down the now-closed book's spine.

"so... she is helping you?" Brendon just nodded, and Declan had to fight the urge to slap him around the head. That was there one advantage, the end of the world didn't know that Billie was helping them and that Felix was back from the future, maybe a little too late for his own good. Declan was looking down at the desk his hands gripping the edges, he didn't know quite how to feel, but the subtle hint of relief that was running through right now was alarming. Something about the fact that Malus knew that Billie was helping them for whatever reason, made him feel like they had an ally in Malus after all Billie was planning on destroying the end of the world, surely that was information malus would be willing to know?

"malus, there is something you should know, the reason Billie is helping us find the evolvers is so she can" he looked up and stared into the red pools of Malus's eyes which were sparked with curiosity "destroy you and the others of the end of the world" The room was silent before a roar of laughter so loud erupted from the immortal's mouth, making both Declan and Brendon flinch violently.

"now that, is funny" he said between gulps of air. "why can't caligo and spiral be as funny as you?"

"no im not joking malus, this is serious stuff", Declan said trying to keep the frustration out of his voice, disrespecting the leader of a villain group wasn't what he wanted to do right now.

"and I, young boy and the absolute master of seriousness. Billie cannot harm us without harming herself that" he clapped his hands together causing for a multiple of the books on the shelves around them to fall to the floor "is the first thing the witches that created us made sure was in place."

He stepped towards them again, his flowing black coat swirling around his legs as he did so. "I don't know why the people of your kind, speak so highly of this place, it is clear they don't teach you anything." Declan was dazed, he could feel the blood in his veins pulse as his heart quickened "so, if Billie tries to destroy you she'll-"

"destroy herself?" Brendon finished, getting to his feet. Malus was just looking at them a smug look set into his chiselled face.

"so that means Billie is sacrificing herself?" Brendon said again, turning to face Declan who was looking past him his eyes locked onto Malus where they held a mutual discovery.

"no Brendon Billie isn't going to try and destroy the end of the world, if she's here trying to help us find the rest of the evolvers then that means she's planning on destroying them-"

Malus was nodding now "before they can destroy us"

* * *

They were trying to kill him. He knew that. What a pity that he actually couldn't be killed. They knew that. Caligo was smiling. The hallways of the academy were bloody, and he sensed that the magic within them was fresh and newly spilt. The muddy footsteps from spiral James's boots mapped his slaughtering journey throughout the academy, and he was sure that whoever was left was either hiding really well or being held captive by Malus. This certainly was a spontaneous turn of events, of course, they brought this on themselves, stealing one of spiral James's inventions was something he didn't take lightly. There was also the fact that Billie and Felix had seemed to have disappeared and the academy had no doubt something to do with that. The white walls looked like pale patches of flesh that had just been slashed with knives, blood was dripping down them and creating pools of blood on the floor, the bodies of the academy members were making it hard to walk in a straight line by the time he reached one of the libraries where a newly laid out massacre was being constructed.

The silence in the room was almost uncomfortable as spiral cleared the head of the last mortal and turned to gave caligo a look that said "go for it" caligo shook his head "drinking the magic from the blood of the mortal you've killed isn't my style im afraid" he said his voice slightly slurred by the saliva that had appeared in his mouth as soon as he smelt the odour of the magic leaking into the room. Spiral just smirked and waved him away as he began to pick the pockets of all the bodies around him. Desperate times, he supposed, as stealing from the magic people was always a pet peeve of spirals which he'd mention every single time caligo did it. Which made him a hypocrite, but of all of the words caligo could think of to describe spiral James, the genius of the end of the world then he guessed that 'hypocrite' was more on the lighter side of things.

❊ ❊ ❊

Malus was pretty sure that his shoelaces were untied. He didn't really think that looking down and retying them if they were was the right thing to do in this situation.

"so what your saying is Billie going to betray us? "Declan was saying, his face unamused and respectfully unsurprised. Malus just smiled at them both blissfully unaware that neither of them knew what was actually happening downstairs.

"what im saying is, young boy is that we are going to betray you" Malus couldn't help the smugness that was potent in his voice, and he saw the blood drain from both of the boys faces as they finally as if someone had pressed the unmute button on the remote, heard the ear-shattering screams coming from their fellow academy members, screams that Malus was sure were only heard in hell, and they seemed to come from every direction as if the wind itself were causing them.

CHAPTER 24
FRIENDS?

After what felt like 2 days, luke had finally caught Ryan up on everything. The end of the world, the elements, how he'd met aria, what had happened to Felix and finally how he had ended up kidnapping Ryan. He hadn't realised how crazy it had all been until he'd been saying out loud and suddenly luke wasn't surprised at the ashen, semi-detached look Ryan had on his face as Luke drove in silence next to him.

The world was dark around them now, and somehow Luke felt like maybe telling Ryan everything was a mistake. He didn't know why but somehow because he knew everything, luke was worried that Ryan no longer needed him.

"say something" Luke said after 5 minutes, it was odd having such a calm reaction to something so big, aria's response was reasonable, valid, right but Ryan just looked like he'd seen a ghost and that wasn't necessarily a good sign.

Ryan just shook his head next to him and managed to croak out "it's insane"

Luke smiled slightly "yes, it is pretty wild"

"so you guys need my help?" Ryan said, a little bit of confidence flooding back into his voice, closely shadowed with surprise.

Luke looked at him briefly "yeah, why do you sound so surprised?"

Ryan looked down "I don't know I guess people don't really see me as someone who can actually do that"

"why not? You're one of the best players in the school, everyone looks up to you"

"yeah but that's only because im good at shooting, no one speaks to me outside of practice. I actually don't even like basketball"

"why do you do it then?"

"it gives me something to channel my anger out on"

Luke nodded. That made sense. "well you won't have to play anymore if you come train with me and the others, trust me punching someone in the face is way better than throwing a ball into a hoop"

"we'll see about that"

"so you want to help?"

"of course, I just don't know what you expect me to do"

"don't worry, im sure Declan will make that very clear to you when we get back"

Ryan just nodded, his hands were clasped together like he didn't know what to do with them. "so am I going to have to go through the same ritual that aria did?" he asked, his voice suddenly mellow and without any intention.

Luke nodded at him, only just remembering that the ritual was a thing and how, without it, he wouldn't be alive today. The cold surface of the table he'd been laying on as he woke up beside aria, still made him shiver every time he thought about it.

"yes but it's not that bad" he said roughly, trying to not sound like that was a lie. He may of not actually been in the ritual to get his powers, but something definitely had changed about him ever since that night, for months now and he still hadn't found out what was wrong.

"wow that was convicing" Ryan said sarcastically, and they both laughed. Luke could only hope that this meant that no police were going to be called and the time for backstabbing, kidnap attempts and ultimately, death was over.

Somehow he couldn't quite believe that.

CHAPTER 25
PITSTOP

T exas was hot. No doubt about it, even at 2am in the morning. Aria was tired. Luckily she hadn't had to drive the whole way as the mini-jet that had been arranged to fly them to America was her sweet escape from it.

She'd slept, of course, and nobody had really spoken until they'd finally touched down in an old, rusty Texan airport. They were now all cramped into an equally as rusty rental car and Aria refused to drive this time.

Alice was at the wheel, and after 5 minutes of driving, everyone aria was sure, was wishing they were driving instead.

"Alice don't you think you should actually use your hands to drive and not your knees," Aria said, trying to keep herself from grabbing the steering wheel herself from where she sat in the passenger seat. Alice was just laughing, and Aria was sure that the lack of sleep had gotten to her.

"You're boring, live a little," she said, throwing her hands up in the air and screaming.

"All I can say is," Billie said from the back seat "that im

sure glad I can't actually die right now"

Aria just turned to look at her and at the same time caught Felix rolling his eyes.

"oi no one is going to die." Alice said death staring them all through the rearview mirror. "You just might not make it back to England with *all* your limbs" she shrugged and smiled a smile that showed her annoyingly perfect straight white teeth.

Aria knew she was safe, well as safe as she could be in the company of an immortal and two of the best trained anti evolvers in the academy, and she of course was an evolver which anyone else but her would class as a gift from god, but Aria just couldn't help but think that she was more of a hindrance than anything remotely good sent from heaven.

They had been sat in the car for a while, and Aria's legs had started to go numb, sleep was weighing her eyelids down, and everyone apart from Billie looked like they could use a nap or two. If Billie could keep a lookout without killing them or letting them get killed, then Aria thought, she could be trusted even just a little tiny bit.

The device in her pocket buzzed then, and she nearly hit her head on the roof of the car to get to it. She saw Alice give her a side look which meant, in Aria's head of Alice based gestures, 'what was that?'. Aria looked down at the matchbox device, all the screen showed was the map of their surrounding area and the dot that signified where the 2nd evolver was. It took Aria a second to realise that the other shape gliding past the dot was them.

She screamed purely because she didn't know what else to do. Before she could even let Alice know what was happening, Aria had yanked at the stirring wheel so that they skidded on the dirt road and did a very messy U-turn to continue on the way they'd just come.

"what the fu-" alice started, slapping Aria's hands off the wheel.

"Alice we just drove *past* them" Aria said trying hard to squint through the darkness at the road trying to see something that looked like a building or a house or something. All she could see though was the outline of a vehicle that looked like a van parked rather haphazardly on the side of the road. Nothing else surrounded it and no one seemed to be in the driver's seat, but something in Aria's blood told her that this was it.

This was where the 2nd evolver was hiding.

* * *

Ryan had needed a wee. Luke had guessed that the number of toilets wasn't high on the desert road that connected one of these dilapidated towns from the other, so he had pulled over and laid in the cool back of the van while Ryan went about his business outside. He was tired, and his body responded to the hard but soothing floor of the van like his brain responded to the thought that maybe, he would be able to see his brother again. He stopped that thought. The tears that had threatened to form dying on his tear ducts like the way sun dries up the rain after a thunderstorm. This wasn't what he needed right now, if he was going to help the others defeat the end of the world then all thought of Felix would need to be gone from his head.

There was a noise outside, and Luke wasn't fazed at first, Ryan had probably just fallen over on his way to get back to their van, but then he heard a voice so clear and un-detachable from the person it belonged too, he sat up, blinking away the tiredness from his eyes and wishing so wholeheartedly that this wasn't a dream.

The voice spoke again, and this time there was no doubt that the words he heard now, the voice that had woven its self into his thoughts ever since he'd last heard it , was the voice he didn't know he needed to hear until now and it carried his tired legs up and out of the van.

* * *

Aria creed had seen some pretty mad stuff over the past few months, no one could deny that but seeing a teen-age boy falling over his own feet trying to avoid touch-ing the body of a rattle snake, was something she was sure wouldn't leave her memory any time soon. They had parked the car behind the body of the van and were just getting out when they'd heard the muffled scream of a boy who didn't want to wee anywhere near an animal that could poison him whole if its heart desired. Alice had approached him, killing the snake and stopping its pursuit of the boy in the process, which left him speech-less and well surely caught in their net of attention.

"what can I do for you lovely ladies?" he asked, blushing slighty. His eyes skimmed Aria's and flowed onto Alice and Billie's completly ignoring Felix, who was failing to hide the laughter that he was trying to contain.

"uh we need you to do something for us?" Alice said, her mouth twisted into a sweet smile.

"oh yeah, what do you need?"

"can you touch this?" Aria asked, reaching into her

pocket.

Ryan frowned slightly at the device in front of him but didn't hesitate to plant his intext finger on the device's screen. "is that it?" his eyebrows were raised and a smirk was appearing slowly onto his face.

"uh yeah I guess, thank you anyway " Aria's heart dropped as she saw that the dot hadn't dissapeared yet. she went to turn back to the car when- "what is taking so long?"

Luke.

It was Luke.

She knew that voice anywhere. He rounded the corner of the van, and she felt the air and the people around her freeze. Her heart seemed to be the only thing that was moving, and she was sure if it didn't slow down, it would break through her chest and end up on the floor. If Ryan wasn't the second evolver then did that mean that some-how luke …

"luke?…. luke" was all she could say as she brought the device out in front of her, the red dot still as prominent as after. she looked at him, at his face, even in the dark-ness she could see the blue of his eyes, the brightness of his hair and that even though she was sure she was wrong, even though it was surely impossible, everything inside her spoke to her, the elements willing her to make the connection.

"you, your- " she stammered, trying desperately to get her words out of her now trembling lips, as if he could sense the same thing she could in the air between him, in a second he was stood in front of her and was touching the device with his whole hand. She closed her eyes, al-most not wanting to see the dot again when she opened them, but Aria wasn't shocked that when she did open her eyes, that she wasn't just looking at the spot on the map where the dot used to be, but when she looked up into Luke's overwhelming blue eyes, she wasn't shocked or even surprised anymore that she was looking into the eyes of the second evolver.

CHAPTER 26
I NEED ANSWERS

L uke was frozen. His fingers were numb. His toes felt like they were part of the array of stones that littered the floor at his feet. His hair was being rubbed softly against his face as the night breeze tried to, it seemed, shift his focus away from his brother.

Felix was standing there, about three meters away. He didn't look scared, he didn't look tortured, and he didn't look *real*.

The fact that no one had mentioned him or even acknowledged that he was there with them make Luke find it hard to believe he wasn't hallucinating. What if he was? and he was just staring at someone, what if it was actually Brendon, he didn't go anywhere without Alice, and the fact that he couldn't see him now would explain a lot, but something was off. Felix was looking at him too, it was the sort of look you gave someone when you weren't quite sure if you should hug them or not and this was the only thing that was stopping luke from running to him now and doing exactly that.

His attention was then drawn to Billie. Who was looking down at her phone, seemingly unaware of the fact that she was even standing with them. She didn't look like she was about to kill anyone and she didn't even look like she was trying to keep Felix hostage but then, everything stopped and as if it was as simple as flowing down a river, his eyes drifted back to Aria. The tears that then started to run down his cheeks surprised him and Aria, as if it was the only thing she knew how to do, hugged him in an embrace that didn't just fill the hole that had been left in his heart for months, but it silenced the doubt in his mind that nothing would be the same again.

"we will explain everything once we get somewhere a little less... sandy" Aria said trying to keep her voice steady and her eyes hopeful, he could tell she was trying hard not to cry too. Whatever had happened while he'd been away was far far worse than anything he'd been imagining.

"uh yeah okay" he said, barely being able to whisper. Everyone was silent, and the look Felix was giving him stung his heart.

❊ ❊ ❊

Aria didn't know if she was dreaming. She didn't know if the heat and the lack of sleep were playing on her mind but how could it be, that Luke, a person that hadn't shown or experienced any signs of being an evolver ever, could be one of the ones that help her in destroying the end of the world. She was thankful that Alice was as upbeat as she was because if she wasn't so happy to see Luke again and so intrigued to meet this mysterious new Ryan boy, there would be a blanket of silence covering them all. Felix was the quietest out of them all, and everyone couldn't help but notice the lack of excitement or love between the two brothers. It was strange, but Aria wasn't surprised to see it, they'd both been through some bad stuff and Felix, especially spending years in a future where mostly everyone was dead.

She didn't feel like talking, the draining sensation she felt from the day weighed down her excitement of seeing luke again and at the same time finding the second evolver. Billie just looked bored which wasn't a surprise and she could tell that she could possibly know more about the situation than any of them, considering the fact that she and Felix had spent more time together than anyone in the past few months.

They were walking to a building on the horizon that Luke had said he's seen when he'd been driving and that it looked like a good place for a catch-up. Even though it was dark and sand was getting into every piece of clothing she was wearing, Aria felt like something wasn't right, she felt restless, and her heart kept going into fits of hammering through her chest. It was making her feel dizzy, and she was grateful when the doorway to the old blacksmiths building that Luke had spotted on the way down, loomed in front of them.

"im not going to sugar coat this but this isn't right" Luke said after they'd all made it inside, finding anything remotely stable to sit on. He looked annoyed which, Aria couldn't blame him for feeling, there was clearly a lot they'd all been hiding from him.

"I don't even know what questions to ask first to get the answers I want so please just someone tell me what the hell happened after I left?" he was looking at Felix, but his words addressed the whole room in a way that made it feel like they were all in the headmaster's office after causing a food fight in the canteen.

Aria cleared her throat at the same time Alice clapped her hands together, both of them clearly wanting to talk.

"so when you left Declan put me and Alice in charge of the academy" Aria said, trying to sound calm and like none of what had happened recently was a big deal. "and we did a banging job if I do say so myself" Alice chipped in raising her eyebrows authoritatively.

"and so nothing happened for two months we were just running patrols and keeping the criminals at bay..." She let her voice trail, something inside her didn't want to tell him about his brothers return.

"but then two weeks ago aria came back from her patrol with a little guest" she gestured towards Felix who was, it was clear to everyone in the room, trying not to make a run for it. He looked shifty, and at that moment, Aria didn't blame luke for being angry. Felix looked like Felix, but it was as clear as day it wasn't the Felix they all knew from before. Luke's eyes just scanned his brother's body as if he was trying to find something he recognised about it

"Felix? What hap-"

"I'm not who I used to be Brother I –"Felix began, finally wiping the ghostly expression from his face.

"he went to the future while trying to get Eddie's body back from the past" Billie said, coming out of the corner she had managed to momentarily disappear into too.

"it was a mistake in spiral James's design, it took him 3 years into the future where he then lived there for another 5 years before we could get him back, luke" she sounded careless, but her face was stern, and Aria thought that this was the most serious she'd ever seen her.

Luke's face looked ashen as he slowly began to understand why his brother seemed so absent. He looked pitiful as he eye'd Felix differently.

"so after Felix returned, Billie shortly followed and offered me an Aria a deal"

"A ... deal?" luke said raising his eyebrows and looking Billie up and down like he wasn't sure if he was happy about that fact or not.

"she would get rid of the criminals if we helped her destroy the end of the world" Aria said, again trying not to look Luke in the eyes, she hadn't realised how insane that sounded until she'd just said it out loud to him. Luke's eyes shifted to her, and she could see that he clearly wasn't impressed.

"you are joking?, those are both things we were going to do anyway and WHY would *she*" he was pointing at her now "want to destroy the end of the world??"

Alice and Aria were silent for a while before Felix spoke from behind them.

"you guys wouldn't understand, the end of the world aren't a team like you guys are, they were put together for a purpose. You have to remember I spent three months with them" he paused, the distant look back in his eyes and Aria knew he was thinking about what came after that.

"then after we brought her back to the academy where she agreed to steal this for us" Aria pulled the matchbox device from her pocket "that's how we found you"

Luke was nodding. Ryan who had been standing almost irrelevant beside him coughed making everyone but Billie jump slightly.

"I'm sorry, but I can't be the only one who finds all of this just a little bit psychopathic?" he looked just as worried as he sounded and Aria couldn't help but feel sorry for him. Billie let out a cracking cascade of laughter before putting her hand over her mouth as if to make it seem less rude.

Alice was smiling at him. "you get used to it after a while, to be honest"

"I'm not" Aria said, crossing her arms together. Ryan just looked at them all, and for a split second, she thought he was going to make a run for it.

"to answer your question, as Felix was saying. We don't actually like each other so why would I want to be a part of that?" Billie continued coughing slightly to cover up her giggles.

"You've been a part of that for thousands of years Billie, it's just strange to me that you suddenly want to destroy them now" Luke said, the distaste clear in his voice.

"because young boy, this has been the only time where you guys are actually getting close to doing it. You have three out of four evolvers what better time than now to switch to the good team?"

"so you're using them?" Ryan said

"uh yes, you clearly haven't met me before"

"so Billie got rid of all the criminals then?" Luke said, returning his inquisitive gaze back to Alice and Aria.

"yes but" Alice began and Aria elbowed her in the ribs before she could finish.

"that's it nothing else has happened" Aria said, trying too not sound suspicious and failing. She could see Alice was staring at her in disbelief and even Felix and Billie looked surprised. Luke pursed his lips together before giving them all an even smile.

"Well thank you for that little storytime. Im afraid my time in America hasn't been all that entertaining apart from finding another evolver to add to our forces"

"new evolver? You mean.." Aria said as everyone looked at Ryan. He flushed suddenly, and this time Alice was the one to burst out laughing.

"he's an evolver?" she asked after she'd finished. Luke looked vaguely annoyed at her outburst but crossed his arms as he said "well im like 80% sure that he is"

"80%?" Alice and Aria said together there unimpressed tones matching.

"well Aria aren't you able to tell? You are one after all?" luke said, almost defensively. Aria just smiled at him, shaking her head slowly from side to side. "no luke because I think you've already done that yourself, as we know for some impossible reason, you are also one. I trust your judgement"

"yeah actually how *is* luke an evolver?" Alice said, her voice growing high pitched as the question in her eyes grew. Luke was just shaking his head,

"I have no idea I guess it must have something to do with –"

" – when you died" Aria finished for him almost automatically because it went along with what she was thinking. Technically luke was dead when they did the evolver ritual on Aria, which could mean that if the evolver ritual was the thing that brought him back to life, could it also be the thing that made him one too? Aria was about to voice these thoughts when the thumping in her chest got suddenly more rapid, and everything around her seemed to go white before she heard the building explode around her.

CHAPTER 27
ALMOST

For some reason, the fact that the floor seemed to disappear from underneath them all wasn't the thing that shocked her. The thing that shocked her was the fact that she wasn't expecting it. Billie wasn't interested in the interaction unfolding in front of her. It was tame, and in the grand scheme of Billie's life, it was pointless like most things. One thing she couldn't help but feel invested in was the fact that they'd found the 2nd evolver.

That just left one more to find. That, however, didn't matter now because somehow, she was pretty sure, the building she was previously just stood in, had just been blown up. There was no sound to accompany this fact only the motion of her body flying through the air, the surrounding architecture of the building turning into shatters around them. She almost smiled as she hit the ground and the familiar figure of caligo was there extending his hand to her. Almost.

His fangs were out, and the moon was outlining the blonde in his hair. " fancy seeing you here" he said as she took his still cold hand. She was sharply pulled to her feet.

" you have good timing" she said, brushing the sand from

her clothes. Billie was aware that the others around them were stirring where they lay on the ground and that if they were gonna ever going to trust her further, she would have to change the intent of this interaction.

" where are malus and spiral?" she asked trying to sound stern and infernal, which wasn't hard.

" they're ... " he paused, almost looking sheepish " around" he said finally. Billie just nodded, fully aware that 'around' meant that it wasn't going to be this calm for long. "your vampires – "

"yeah, don't start Billie, they've got a mind of there own at the moment" he paused again, this time a grin spread across his face "not that im complaining"

" I bet you're not" she muttered, trying not to look like she was enjoying the chaos of the now ruined building around her. It wasn't so much the destruction that had been caused that thrilled her so much, it was the way it felt to watch the walls, the ceilings and the foundation of something that was once so strong could be destroyed so easily. It reminded her somewhat of the world and the mortals within it.

" of all the places you could have run off too, you run off *here*" malus was stood behind her. She didn't have to turn around to know, he wasn't pleased with her, He radiated frustration and Billie guessed that for the first time in a long time he'd hadn't a clue what was going on. Billie turned only aware that she had a boot missing from her foot when a sharp stone jabbed into the side of her little toe.

"better than being holed up in that stingy little dungeon of yours," she said, finally turning to see him. He looked mildly less pale than expected, and his coat was covered in something that smelt vaguely of petrol. His eyes were sparkling, and the red inside them seem to set alight as he moved them to look at the mess behind her. He smiled then.

" caligo what have you done?" he asked, his tone requesting that no one needed to answer. As he moved to get a closer look, he revealed the sunset behind him. It glowed but with nowhere near the same brightness of the burning building behind them or the eyes of spiral James as he dropped to the ground in front of her, two blades in his hands.

Billie could only gasp as one was plunged into her chest. The blade stung as it entered and then was ripped out of her unbeating heart. Up until that point, she'd thought the Texan sun had been the hottest thing her skin had ever felt, but she knew then, as the wound opened that her blood was, in fact, a million times hotter.

❊ ❊ ❊

Aria knew two things. One was that they weren't having an innocent catch up anymore, and the other was that she was no longer breathing. She could feel the air building up in her chest, and at some point, it felt like her lungs would explode. She could hear faint voices in the background, nothing she could or even wanted to pay attention too, the pain in her chest, in her body in fact. Everything felt hot, and it took her a few seconds to realise that something was laying on top of her. It was burning her skin slightly, the air around her was only slightly cooler, and the smell of smoke and burning wood was slowly beginning to fill her nostrils. Aria sensed that something had gone horribly wrong, which seemed a little stupid now to think as obviously something *had* , the building they were once in was on fire and debris was laying on top of her. She didn't even want to think about the state the others were in.

* * *

Eddie couldn't move, his eyes were open, and he was staring at the night sky, trying to allow his brain to comprehend what had just happened. It was strange being on the end of an attack that he once used to be the one carrying out, but those days were a long time ago now. That didn't stop him, however knowing that the end of the world had found them and they weren't, understandably happy with them. His eyes were watering as the smoke from the burning building around him clouded his peripheral vision. His body didn't hurt, he was too numb, and the slight feeling of the wind blowing his hair onto his face was almost enough to calm his rapidly beating heart. Almost.

he moans of Luke Quinn near him brought his attention back from looking at the stars. It was odd to Eddie, the feeling of having to pretend to care about someone they used to despise so much. Of course, spending the time he did in the future with him made their dynamic change. Still, the pain Eddie had felt when he'd seen Luke for the first time since the place he'd seen him die 8 years on into the future, was the same if not more than any hurt pain a real brother could feel. But this wasn't the Luke Quinn 8 years into the future, the Luke Quinn who knew who he really was.

He could see or sense someone moving next to him, the

smell of blood was almost overwhelming, and the metallic taste was almost enough to sting his tongue.

There was a commotion going on somewhere behind him, but his attention was still focused on the body of luke next to him. It was moving slowly, and Eddie had to hold his breath to make out the words he was saying in deep, withdrawn whispers.

" Felix? Felix I –" he began, his words were then drowned out by a huge slab of ceiling breaking apart from the roof and falling just a few inches from both of them. Eddie was too dizzy to even register how close it had come to squashing them, the pain all of his body felt like fuzzy liquid moving around so much he couldn't pinpoint where on his body was actually hurt.

" Felix?" it was luke again, his voice more audible and full of life. Eddie could only just about muster a groan in response before oddly cold stong hands were on him, pulling him slowly to his feet. He didn't know how luke had gotten up so quick or even if he had, his eyes were barely able to open. He felt his eyes lull to the back of his head as another pair of hands gripped his waist, keeping him from falling down. They were moving now, and it was odd because he could still hear luke's voice, but as he moved, it got further and further away. Eddie managed to turn his head slightly so his slightly closed eyes could see, to his absolute horror, that the hands gripping his arms weren't that of luke Quinn. But those of Caligo Bellator and next to him, spiral james.

* * *

Luke just hoped he was dreaming. He sure felt like he was. He couldn't remember how but he'd managed to get himself free from the tangle of debris and wood he'd been laying in and now he was slumped frozen by shock by the body of Aria creed. She wasn't breathing that was a definite and her limbs and torso were slashed from the pieces of building stuck into them. He felt sick, and he felt like he couldn't breathe. Luke knew she was an evolver, and she would be able to heal herself but did that rule still apply when her heart wasn't being allowed to beat?

His body felt numb, and he willed for his body to move to hers and push the debris off her chest so she could breathe again. But he couldn't his hands were shaking and his head felt like it was filled with cement. Luke suddenly looked up as he sensed someone approaching from behind him, his hands went to his belt trying to reach for his dagger, but of course, it wasn't there.

He was too slow and too weak to stop the hands that grabbed him and started to pull him away from Aria. Another figure was by her, and he felt a wave of relief hit him as she was lifted like she weighed nothing, all the bits of wood and concrete gone from her body now. Luke almost smiled as he realised that she would be able to heal now.

Almost.

His attention was brought back to the person currently dragging him, he felt cold, but the strength in his arms made luke feel like he was made of nothing. He didn't feel panicked just numb to everything, even the sight of the burning, dilapidated building he was being taken away from. Even though there was fire everywhere, he still felt cold, and he wasn't sure now if he was shaking because of shock or shivering because of the cold. Suddenly he wasn't moving anymore, and he was falling. He hit the ground on his knees, his hands flying out to brace him. His eyes were watering, but he could see clear as day then the four pairs of feet that were lined up before him.

His body seemed to stop then, stop shivering, stop thinking as it all suddenly made sense. The end of the world had found them.

Luke noticed then as all of his senses seemed to sharpen that Felix, Aria and Ryan were all on there knees next to him, seemly all in the same state of shock he was in. Still, they weren't looking around there eyes were set on a place he hadn't looked at yet. He felt his eyes shift so that now he was looking and sharing in the utter new wave of sickness he felt in his stomach as he saw Billie's body slumped just a few metres away from where the end of the world were lining up. A blade was the only thing keeping her upright, and a growing pool of blood was encircling her. Her eyes looked distant as she wasn't dead just growing weaker and luke couldn't help the strange sense of sadness he felt looking at her in such a vulnerable form. As If malus could see the utter horror in all of their eyes then, he spoke addressing them all.

" that is what happens, my children, to lairs" His voice seemed to vibrate through him, it seemed to boom around the ruins of the building and circle back to him with extra vengeance. He chuckled

" now you may be wondering 'what would I have against lairs?' I am one right?" he was pacing around them now his voice fluctuating in Luke's ears.

" I don't care that she lied to me, I don't even care that she helped you" luke could see Felix next to him shaking his head slightly, his lips were moving, but no sound seemed to leave them.

" no, I just think it's a real shame that the truth, something you guys seem to be so keen on telling, shouldn't be kept from you. Im doing you a favour when I say that Billie has been lying to you but" he laughed again this time it reminded luke of a cheeky schoolboy. It made him shiver.

" that's not the best part, not only has Billie been lying to you but your beloved Felix Quinn has told the biggest lie of the century" Luke felt his stomach dropped as he looked at his brother. Malus was crouching now, next to Felix's kneeing figure, his hands gripping at the roots of Felix's stalk black hair so that he was forced to look malus in the eyes.

" why don't you tell them, Felix? Or should I say..." Luke was almost sure it looked like malus was smiling, but then again, he was almost sure he'd never felt this level of confusion before. What could Felix have lied about? To him? To aria? To the academy? He held his breath as malus looked up so his voice could be heard for the final word of his sentence.

"Eddie"

CHAPTER 28
EDDIE

Even with the fuzzy static ringing in her ears, Billie heard the name. It seemed to cut through all the pain and clear her mind of all its fogginess. There was a sword shoved through her chest, granted it wasn't just any sword. It was a special sword designed to harm and weaken immortals. Of course, it was.

She just hoped that the evolvers never learned of this weapon as it could very possibly be the end of the world's downfall. She opened her eyes, just in time to see the shocked and hurt faces of the academy members in front of them. Eddie was shaking his head, and even from where she knelt in the lowlight of the morning, she could still see the faint glimmer of his tears as they fell from his eyes.

No one was talking except Malus who seemed to never shut up. Billie was trying to focus. Trying to bring everything in her line of sight back and the milky edge of her mind in so it was sharp again. As far as she was aware, no one was talking. If they were, she wouldn't be able to hear them over the ringing and roaring in her ears, that had suddenly just become apparent to her. She wasn't in pain, yet and she tried to move her hand to brush her fridge from in front of her eyes. It took longer than she would've liked, but eventually, she had a clearish view of the scene in front of her. Really had a view of it because now everyone was standing, weakly but standing all the same.

Aria was looking at her and Billie could've sworn she saw all life die from her eyes so now they were cold, and the glare she was receiving was equally as chilling. Was Billie supposed to pick a side? She had her own agenda to think about. Her own benefits for keeping Aria and her friends alive but she wasn't in a position to fight against Malus and whoever decided to stand with him. It was clear from just looking at the scene in front of them that something was about to happen and as much as Billie wanted too, she couldn't let the magic people die, not just yet.

So as much as she knew this could affect her in more ways than one, she closed her eyes, allowing for her dreamy state to grow from just beyond her and fuel and run its way to the broken bodies of Aria and Felix.

Billie just hoped they had sweet dreams.

❋ ❋ ❋

The world seemed to shift, and at first, Aria couldn't place why. The earth beneath her almost didn't feel real the hot burn of the morning sun didn't feel so rough on her skin anymore. Aria knew she hadn't been alone, but yet in her hazy field of vision, she could see no one around her. No one except Felix, no, Eddie. She almost felt dumb for even being convinced they were the same, in the dark depths of her heart she had known, of course, the truth.

Felix from the future or not, nothing could ever keep

luke and him apart. She knew that, they all did and was she meant to believe that Eddie had really changed?

Really had the future made him see how bad the end of the world would be? But how could she not believe that when she'd seen the absolute wallowing sadness in his eyes whenever he spoke of the events to come. He was looking at her, and it was weird that that was the first thing she noticed when all around them was white.

Aria couldn't place what the whiteness was or why it was calming her, slowly so that her heart was no longer angrily beating in her chest. Was she dead? It sure looked and felt like it, she felt numb too, and the whiteness was almost blinding like someone was shinning stadium floodlights into her eyes.

Felix – no Eddie, was looking equally as dumfounded, Were they both dead? He had started to walk towards her now, and it surprised her oddly, that whatever the whiteness was beneath them, however much it looked like clouds, was solid enough to be a concrete pavement. As he neared, Aria could see something in his stolen eyes that was something close to sorrow. There were no tears, but the sadness she felt just by looking into his face was almost enough for her to feel sorry for him.

His lips were moving, and she had to focus on them to actually hear the words he was saying.

" are you okay? Aria?" his tone was soft, yet it still smacked her hard, like she'd walked into a wall. She couldn't help but smirk at him, she felt the sarcasm rise Inside her because after all, how could she possibly be okay after any of this?

" what do you think Felix?" she stopped, her cheeks threatening to go red, how could she be embarrassed about that? " Eddie, whoever you are"

" come on Aria, you're not yourself, this isn't you" he was frowning at her, his eyes twinkling.

Rage.

Rage flared up in her eyes, in her mind, and she couldn't stop her hand from connecting with his cheek, with a slap so hard it left his skin red and sore. He flinched, and she saw the momentary blink of surprise run across his face.

" you don't get to talk to me about being myself"

" aria, I was just trying to –"

" Eddie, whatever you say now, cannot, will not fix the fact that Felix, the *real* one, is not here"

"everything that I've seen aria cannot excuse the fact that you don't know what you're talking about"

" oh really? Eddie, you pretended to be Felix, you pretended to be one of us, you pretended to be my friend, I think I do know what im talking about"

"Aria that's what you don't understand, I've lived in Felix's body, as Felix, for eight years. After a while, I stopped pretending, and it's not like you didn't have some suspicions"

" so you're blaming me for this?"

"it's not like I was trying to be Felix, I was trying to be a new Eddie, an Eddie that has fallen in love with this magic, with your world I have Felix's magic in my veins im not evil Eddie that's part of the end of the world anymore, spending time with you in the future has changed me and im-" he paused " im scared of what the others will do to me when they find out"

Aria looked at him then, like she was finally putting it all into focus.

" find out what exactly? " she asked him. He sighed almost as if he'd wished he hadn't said anything.

" if Malus or even Billie find out that I don't want to get rid of magic, that I actually like this world, they would –" he broke off an aria couldn't help but see plain as day, the fear in his eyes. Aria still couldn't forgive him. How could she, she felt the anger twisting inside her, and she knew it would be a matter of time before it was going to erupt out of her like lava overflowing a dormant volcano.

" Eddie, that still doesn't change the fact that you lied and you have to realise how unfair it is to pretend to be Felix, Lukes brother, my friend–" she stopped, a dawning realisation striking her.

"Eddie," she said softly, her voice shaking under the overwhelming pressure of the very possibility her realisation had. Before he could answer, however, figures started to appear all around them in the white haze. Luke and Ryan's faces emerged at first and then Alice's and finally Billie's still ashen from the blood loss. There was a silence and Aria couldn't help but stare at the red iris's that was the only things on Billie's body that still had any real colour. She smiled weakly as if she was reading Aria's thoughts.

" you think im to blame for this?" she said sharply

" well yes, how can we trust you when you forgot to tell us that Eddie took over Felix's body seconds before he died"

" if he took over Felix's body then—" luke started and then broke off quickly as he had the same realisation that Aria had had minutes before. They all looked at Billie questioningly. She was holding her breath, but she didn't look remotely threatened as she said her next words that felt cold and dead in Aria's ears.

" Felix is dead, yes"

Aria closed her eyes. The blackness behind them was calming in contrast to the bright and now erratic light of the whiteness they were standing in. she breathed in, trying to stop the anger that was building, the hurt that was brewing and the tears that were threatening to fall. Her lips were numb, and she formed the only words her brain could comprehend

" what the hell " she whispered hoarsely, her throat was dry. She swallowed slowly before opening her eyes again. " you can't expect us to trust either you anymore" she stepped away from Eddie almost as a reflex to her words and luke gripped and her shoulders gently.

" I just saved you from all getting killed" Billie said dryly. " none of this would've of happened Billie if you would've just told us the truth!" Aria screamed suddenly. "whoa, why are you blaming me when it was Eddie's lie and Eddie's problem"

"oh trust me im blaming Eddie just as much"

" frankly I don't care, all I care about is getting my brother back. And don't say he's dead beacuse I know you immortals have something that could work and I don't know about everyone else but im willing to do anything." Aria nodded along with Ryan and Alice at luke's words.

Billie rolled her eyes " I do have an idea, but Im not sure you're gonna like it."

CHAPTER 29
IT'S NOT OVER YET.

J ust like that, they were back at the academy. No long
drives, no secret plane journeys that made her head
feel like it wanted to explode. In just a blink of an
eye they all appeared in the west wing library which
was dark and dimly lit by warm lamps that hung from
the walls. It was nighttime outside, and everyone stayed,
oddly silent. There was something strange about this
room and Aria couldn't put her finger on it, there was a
clinging coldness that seemed to not want to leave her
alone. And she shivered as the coldness spread, uninvited
into her gut as she realised what it meant. She had felt
it when she'd arrived at the prison, she had felt it on her
patrols, she had felt it when she'd laid by Lukes side, the
ever-present, unnerving coldness of death.

Aria's eyes reluctantly went to the floor, the lamplight
barely reached the crimson red carpet. Still, even in the
low light, it wasn't hard to see the sprawled, stretched
out bodies of the Texan clan. Their blood blending into
their surroundings. She felt too frozen to scream, her
mind was frantically flicking through all the possibilities
and all the consequences of this. Declan? Brendon? The
other members of the academy? Were they alive? Who
could of done this?. But as the others started protesting

in weakened cries and sobs around her, it was clear to her, to them all who, or whom had done this.

The end of the world were messing with them. Taunting them. And it just made the burning passion of anger and hatred for Billie and Eddie next to her, ever so pungent.

This needed to end.

* * *

Her hands were still shaking as she washed them under the cold water in the sink. Her chest felt tight and she wanted to punch something. If alice were here she would've told Aria to go ahead but she wasn't here and Aria liked the mirror she was currently looking at herself in, breaking it wouldn't be very helpful.

She felt sick. She needed to talk to someone but she didn't know who, she wanted to say something but she didn't know what and most importantly she wanted to do something but she didn't know what she could do to fix this.

They had 3 evolvers. That was good. The ideal logical next step would be to find the 4th. Still, every time she thought of that scenario, a burning pang of guilt and sadness washed over her because Felix still wasn't here. There was only one person who would understand and she was about to leave the bathroom to go get him when someone knocked at her bedroom door. She crossed the room and opened it, not hiding the smile that graced her lips when she saw the soft blonde hair and beautiful blue eyes of luke Quinn and beside him stood Ryan his eyes fixed on the scar resting on her cheekbone.

"hi aria, sorry if we're disturbing you, but I just thought you should meet Ryan properly" She nodded, still smiling. " of course, please come in"

* * *

Luke was always surprised at how messy Aria's room could get. Every time he was in here, it seemed to progressively get more and more untidy, and today was no different. She was sat on her bed, her head in her hands and luke and Ryan were sat on the two armchairs that were placed in the corner before the window. They had told her the story of how they met and luke's time in America which had ended in a brief question and answer session before Aria had gone back to her thoughts.

" you know what we have to do now Luke, don't you?" she said after a few minutes.

He did. They all did. And he knew nothing was going to stop him in making sure it was done. He looked down at his hands, at his bitten nails and at his dry, sunburnt fingers.

" yes, aria. We're going to get Felix back"

"but Billie said he was dead?" Ryan said from beside him. Aria seemed to flinch away from his words and luke just shook his head at him. "you'll soon realise that in this world, dead doesn't mean you'll stay that way"

"Aria, Billie can help us, she's the only one who can. We've just gotta make sure we keep her in line and keep ourselves in control."

Aria was nodding her eyes resting on his.

"when we get Felix back, we find the 4th evolver and we kill every last one of them" Luke smiled grimly.

"Sounds good, aria creed, that sounds very good to me"

* * *

They were all in the meeting room. The same meeting room Alice hated. It was 3am and nobody looked happy. Nobody *was* happy. Aria was whispering something to luke and he was nodding, his eyebrows furrowed in worry. Even though no one had said what the meeting was about, they all knew it was going to be about getting Felix back and fast.

Alice, despite her hatred towards luke's brother, found herself itching to get a rescue mission formed. It wasn't that she missed him, it wasn't that she had even remotely started to like Felix in his absence, it was the fact that nothing felt the same without him. Alice hated that.

" lets start with the facts" she began seeing as no one else was going to start. she looked at Aria, then to Billie and finally, her eyes rested on Eddie. Felix's eyes stared back, pity practically dripping off them like tears. Billie spoke, her voice dipped in something Alice would like to think was compassion.

" Eddie is in Felix's body, Felix is dead, gone, but if you want to get him back, there is a way" she had her eyebrows raised. A smile was lighting up her face in the sort of way a candle illuminates a pumpkin carving. Luke stood, almost dizzily and Aria put her arm on his to steady him. " what do we have to do?" he asked the immortal. The room seemed to swell, so the walls and all the space in between them grew so the words Billie spoke next echoed in everyone's ears.

CHAPTER 30
ONE SHOT

A s evil as Billie was, she disliked sneaking into places. Especially places that were inhabited by people she also disliked. The end of the world's base was top secret of course, so leading a group of her former enemies to it was more challenging than what was previously thought.

But she had done it, and now her, aria, Alice, Luke, Declan and Ryan were all standing around spiral James's secret time machine, In spiral James's secret lab.

"So how does it work?" Luke asked, running his hand along its metal interior.

"When you and Aria go through it will take you to a time that you're both thinking about," she said, trying to make her voice sound mildly enthused.

"so we both need to think about the exact same time-stamp for this to work," aria said, her eyebrows fur-rowed.

"yes" Billie nodded, why was it so hard to understand?.

"what timestamp would be best to catch Felix at?"

"before we jump out the helicopter," luke said after some thought. Aria just nodded. She had gone pale, and Billie was amused at how mundane and simple the fear in both their eyes was.

"you won't have long, 2 minutes or so max"

"or so?" alice retorted "great so your not even sure how long they get?"

"do you want to get Felix back or not?"

The machine was starting to hum and even from here she could feel the heat radiating from it cylinder shell.

"if you don't make it back in time, that's it, no coming back for you" Now they all looked pale. Ryan looked the most like he wanted to go home, and Billie had to stop herself from shouting 'boo' at him.

Instead, she went over to the time machine and opened its two rouned doors, inside shone a blueish portal that seemed to burn hotter the longer she looked at it. Billie smiled, it looked more beautiful every time.

* * *

The portal was a sizzling rectangle formed by its metal exterior. Aria jumped as electric sparks spat from it.

"it's now or never" Luke said from beside her. He grabbed her hand, and she squeezed it. None of them knew what was about to happen. What they were about to walk into. But she didn't feel scared, just determined to do it right. Alice, Ryan and Declan were all saying stuff behind her. Still, her eyes seem to block everything out except the gentle hum of the machine like it was calling out to her. Luke was still holding her hand, and without thinking, she yanked him forward so they both, fluently as one, went through the portal.

* * *

Luke was back in the helicopter. The wind rushing in his ears, and his hair was blowing off his face. He wasn't in a seat but sprawled at the back with the spare parachutes. He saw himself sitting there next to his brother, a sharp pang of sadness jabbed him. They both suddenly got up, and Luke realised they were approaching the prison and were about to jump into the roof. He just hoped aria was around to catch Felix when they jumped in time.

He saw the figures of himself, Declan and Felix jump from the moving helicopter and a wave of relief hit him as he saw the blur of aria swooping by and snatching Felix mid-air before he could land on the roof. It took luke a second to realise that the helicopter was lowering and that any second it was going to crash into the trees. if he didn't move now, he would add to the wreckage and his hair looked too good today to let that happen.

CHAPTER 31
TIME WAITS FOR NO ONE, NOT EVEN ARIA CREED.

Alice hated waiting. She was impatient and the fact that she might not even see luke an aria again if they didn't make it back within the 2 mins, wasn't helping her with the anxiety that seemed to crowd her mind.

She couldn't sit down, she didn't want to talk to anyone, and that had created an uneasy silence in the room that no one wanted to break. She looked at her phone, they had a minute and a half left. Great.

Declan was lighting and relighting a small flame in his hands, and Alice was slowly becoming mesmerised with it. He looked at her bemused, and she scowled at him, turning her attention to Ryan who was checking out some of spiral James's lab equipment.

"if you break anything, you do realise the punishment will be far worse than 60-minute detention after school" she said, trying to inject some lightheartedness into her voice. Still, instead, her words fell flat, and he just looked at her eyebrows raised.

"I bet you don't even know what half this stuff is," he said, coming over to show her something that had a million tiny tubes coming out of it.

"and you do?" she asked him, not caring but glad to have something to take her mind of the one minute her friends had remaining to come back alive.

"yeah, this is all really rare stuff, and it's so-"He stopped as Billie came over and snatched the thing Ryan was holding in his grip out of his hands and placed it forcefully back on the table.

"don't touch," she said gruffly. Ryan gulped and looked down as Alice smiled weakly, upset that she was too stressed to have enjoyed that moment for what it was. Alice looked at her phone again. Ten seconds. Nine seconds Eight seconds, Seven, six, five, four, three, two...

One.

She looked up eagerly, expecting to see a shape or a movement in the shimmering surface of the portal. Still, her heart sank to the very bottom of her soul as no one came through. Not even Felix.

❊ ❊ ❊

Aria was falling, the body of a sprawling Felix Quinn in her grip. He was yelling, screaming thrashing but Aria was holding onto him as hard as she could. He smelt of smoke and as they hit the ground rolling, she headbutted him in the shoulder, causing herself to cry out in pain and release him. He rolled and got to his knees, his daggers out looking at her furiously. But his eyes softened as he saw her, still laying on the ground, breathing heavily.

"Aria? What are you-"

"shhh we don't have time you need to come with me-"she

got up, looking around at the line of trees they were near, the prison was 30 meters away in the centre of the circle of trees they were standing in. she could see the figures of herself and the others on top of the roof. Time was running out. She knew it. But where was luke ?

"what do mean? You were just on the roof and –"he stopped as Aria punched him square in the nose. He dropped to the floor and Aria grabbed his fallen dagger and put it in her own belt.

"sorry Felix but we're gonna have to save your welcome back speech for later" She squinted as she saw luke running towards them, over the grass his clothes slightly burnt and his hair windswept. She grabbed Felix, picked him up just as he made it to her side, he took his brother without saying a word.

A blue flash exploded in front of her as the portal re-appeared just a few metres away from then, luke ran over to it and placed the body of Felix through it before standing and waiting for Aria to join him. And she was about to join him when something in the tree line flashed and caught her eye.

She peered closer, her eyes honing in on the girl standing still, staring straight at her. Aria didn't move, and her body went numb all of a sudden because the girl seemed too familiar to her yet so strange. They were looking at each with an understanding, but Aria wasn't sure what it was yet. She was aware of luke shouting at her from where he was standing, but nothing else seemed to matter but the draw and her sudden willingness to go to the girl. Her legs wouldn't move but as Lukes cries grew louder, so did the voice in her head that told her to approach the girl. She was about to take her step when she was ripped away from the soft beckoning vision of the girl and flung by strong, strong hands in the direction of the already closing portal, luke was ahead of her and running, her legs felt like jelly, and she knew any second they were about to give out on her, luke reached the portal and jumped through, it was only her now, no one could save her if she didn't make it. She breathed heavily, trying to get the muscles in the legs to wake up. She knew she only had a few seconds left until the portal closed.

Still, She had at least 5 meters to go so she bit her lip, summoning every ounce of strength she had left, holding her hands out and willing the wind to lash onto her. Aria leapt high into the air and swooped down, hitting the ground rolling until she heard the portal and the distinguishing zap it made as it closed forever.

CHAPTER 32
WELCOME BACK

F elix hadn't wanted to wake up. The pressure that had multiplied as soon as he'd become aware that he wasn't where he once was, was almost enough to make him pass out again. He'd tried to open his eyes, but the light that greeted him was blinding, and he wondered then if he was dead. The last thing he remembered was jumping out of Declan's helicopter and falling to the ground – no, someone – Aria catching him and then – A slicing pain ran across his forehead as his brain struggled to remember the events beyond that and to give them an understanding.

This all felt wrong, miss placed somehow, and he felt sick, and oddly jet lagged which just confused him even more. His ears were popping now, and the tingling feeling in his hands and feet did nothing but reassure him that he wasn't dead. But if he wasn't dead and he wasn't still at hill view prison, where the hell was he? He groaned without really meaning too, and his eyes fluttered open, the light not as bright anymore so he could see to his relief that he was in the academy's medical ward with aria's, luke's, Declan's and strangely Alice's faces all looking down at him with worried and concerned expressions on there faces which only made him even more nervous.

What had happened? Why was he here? He didn't feel injured or hurt or even remotely harmed.

"Felix?" luke said, his tone addressing like he wasn't sure if it was really him.

"Luke what's going on why am I –"

"its okay Felix," Luke said softly, and Felix didn't like how warm and Lethargic he was being, now they were all looking at him with sympathy.

"we have a lot to explain to you, you see, you've been gone for three months."

CHAPTER 33
A TINY TEASPOON AMOUNT

Aria was having another meeting. *Yay.* They were becoming a hobby and not one she enjoyed, this one was different. This one was celebratory, but even though they had two members of the end of the world attending, it felt oddly like good news was all they had.

"Eddie, Billie. We can't trust you. But that doesn't mean we don't need you." She said looking at them both from where they sat at the other end of the room. "you need us and that is the only reason you are being allowed to stay" she had her arms crossed and couldn't help but feel like a mother telling her kids they weren't grounded anymore, she didn't like it.

"aria, I haven't been allowed to fully explain myself – " Eddie broke off as she held her hand up to silence him. Eddie was someone she didn't want to speak too.

Eddie and her needed to have a conversation he was right about that. Still, aria had other things on her mind, like the fact that Felix was about two more apologies away from getting fed to the vampires that were still populating most of the city. But they didn't talk about it. They weren't going to talk about it because aria only wanted to hear good news for the rest of the day. She was sick of hearing all the wrong things.

"anyway, Billie we thank you in helping us getting Felix back and for that, you have gained a little tiny, teaspoon amount of our trust"

"speak for yourself" alice muttered from behind her and aria sighed "a little tiny teaspoon amount of *my* trust"

Billie just shrugged and nodded once, unbothered. "now onto more exciting things. Its time to see where the 4th evolver is" she waited as luke handed her the matchbox device. She looked at the screen, and the room was silent as they watched it operate. It beeped as it found the location and butterflies surfaced in her stomach once again. Aria creed looked down at the screen, her hands shaking as she held the device so everyone could see the blinking red dot.

She smiled, now *this* was good news.

EPILOUGE

It was a cold day in Birmingham. The rain was crying tears of the late afternoon down the window. Faye Clarke smiled to herself, that would make a good song lyric, and she quickly wrote it down on the pad of sticky notes that added it to the array she already had covering her desk. The recording studio she was in was big, the biggest one in Birmingham in fact but not the biggest she'd ever been in. She had the choice to record in LA, New York even in abbey road in London. Still, there was just something about recording her music in the hometown that made her feel alive.

She sat back in her chair and stretched, she'd had a long day signing copies of her new album and leading focus groups to see what her fans thought of her unique sound. It was uplifting and finally being able to share her new music with her most devoted fans made for a happy happy happy Faye.

There was a muted knock at the door, and shelly came in, who was her manager and best friend. She swung round to face her, a cup of tea in hand.

"sorry too disturb, are you busy?" she asked, a worried

expression on her face.

"Nah I was just finishing, why? Is something wrong?"

Shelly smiled "good, there are just some fans who wanted to see you they couldn't make the focus group earlier, you don't have to be long"

Fraye smiled at her "of course, let me just pack some stuff up and ill be right down."

"Okay, they'll be in the green room"

* * *

After a few minutes, Faye made her way down to the green room, it wasn't far only a few doors down, and she opened the door to find four people standing talking amongst themselves. They stopped as she walked in and smiled at her. There were two boys and two girls and every single one of them looked like they lived in a gym, muscles bulge under every piece of there clothing and they all gave off an over buzzed 'a never tired sort of vibe'.

"Faye Clarke, we're so excited to meet you" the one with the red hair spoke first her voice made her out to be from down south.

"nice to meet you too, sorry you couldn't make the focus group"

"we underestimated the traffic" the blacked haired boy spoke now, his voice thick with an Irish accent. She nodded, smiling at them. As odd as they seemed, Faye doubted they were serial killers so refrained from calling in Arron her bodyguard in from downstairs.

"im sorry, we haven't introduced ourselves." The red-haired one spoke again. She pointed to the browned haired girl, who looked like she didn't want to be here "this is Alice Taylor, next to her is Felix Quinn and this is luke Quinn, his brother"

"nice to meet you all" she said, failing to understand why she felt like she was being interviewed for a job. She fought the urge to shake there hands.

" im sorry Faye but we have to insist you come with us" the redhead spoke again suddenly stepping forward and seizing her by her wrists.

"what are you doing I will-"

"I wouldn't suggest screaming, or alice will kick you in the ribs, she hates your music"

"what?" Faye was struggling, but this girls strength was impossible to shift .

"who are you?"

The red-haired girl stopped tying her hands to together and looked up, so they're eyes met, hers were a menacing green that seemed to pierce into hers.

"my name is aria creed, it's nice to finally meet you"

Printed in Great Britain
by Amazon

59429691R00129